P9-AGI-631

Again? *Rico had already been married?*

Even in the midst of her turmoil Bella was struck by that unexpected revelation.

"So, if you are cherishing some pitiful fantasy of Cinderella catching her prince, let me assure you that even a pregnancy wouldn't persuade me to make that ultimate sacrifice!"

Bella studied her tightly clenched hands. "You're not my prince, Rico. Relax. Learn to enjoy life as the toad who didn't deserve to be kissed and transformed. This particular Cinderella doesn't believe in fairy tales."

LYNNE GRAHAM was born in Northern Ireland and has been a keen romance reader since her teens. She is very happily married with an understanding husband, who has learned to cook since she started to write! Her three children keep her on her toes. She has a very large Old English sheepdog, which knocks everything over, and two cats. When time allows, Lynne is a keen gardener.

Books by Lynne Graham

HARLEQUIN PRESENTS

Don't miss any of our special offers. Write to us at the following address for information on our newest releases.

Harlequin Reader Service
U.S.: 3010 Walden Ave., P.O. Box 1325, Buffalo, NY 14269
Canadian: P.O. Box 609, Fort Erie, Ont. L2A 5X3

LYNNE GRAHAM

Prisoner of Passion

Harlequin Books

TORONTO • NEW YORK • LONDON
AMSTERDAM • PARIS • SYDNEY • HAMBURG
STOCKHOLM • ATHENS • TOKYO • MILAN
MADRID • WARSAW • BUDAPEST • AUCKLAND

If you purchased this book without a cover you should be aware
that this book is stolen property. It was reported as "unsold and
destroyed" to the publisher, and neither the author nor the
publisher has received any payment for this "stripped book."

ISBN 0-373-11864-3

PRISONER OF PASSION

First North American Publication 1997.

Copyright © 1996 by Lynne Graham.

All rights reserved. Except for use in any review, the reproduction or
utilization of this work in whole or in part in any form by any electronic,
mechanical or other means, now known or hereafter invented, including
xerography, photocopying and recording, or in any information storage
or retrieval system, is forbidden without the written permission of the
publisher, Harlequin Enterprises Limited, 225 Duncan Mill Road,
Don Mills, Ontario, Canada M3B 3K9.

All characters in this book have no existence outside the imagination of
the author and have no relation whatsoever to anyone bearing the same
name or names. They are not even distantly inspired by any individual
known or unknown to the author, and all incidents are pure invention.

This edition published by arrangement with Harlequin Books S.A.

® and TM are trademarks of the publisher. Trademarks indicated with
® are registered in the United States Patent and Trademark Office, the
Canadian Trade Marks Office and in other countries.

Printed in U.S.A.

CHAPTER ONE

HEADS turned when Bella walked down the street. Her rippling mane of Titian curls, her incredibly long legs and her outrageous hotchpotch of colourful clothes caught the eye. But it was her prowling, graceful stride and the light of vibrant energy in her face which made the attention linger. Bella always looked as if she knew exactly where she was going.

She lifted the public phone off the hook and punched in the number. 'Griff?'

'Bella, I'm so sorry...something's come up,' he groaned. 'I have to go back into the office.'

'But—' Her clear eyes froze as she heard a woman giggling somewhere in the background. Griff went on talking, although there was a similar catch of amusement in his voice. Apologising, he assured her that he would be in touch.

Five minutes later Bella was back in the wine bar with her friends.

'Where have you been?' Liz hissed, under cover of the animated conversation.

'Calling Griff...'

'You mean he's not on his way yet?'

Bella gave a careless shrug.

'He's let you down, hasn't he?' her friend said bluntly.

Bella didn't trust herself to speak. And the very last thing she needed right now was a lecture on the subject of Griff Atherton, who was everything Gramps had ever told her to look out for in a man but who was inexplicably as unreliable as they came, in spite of his good education, steady job and stable family background.

5

'You really know how to pick them,' Liz lamented. 'Why do you always latch on to the creeps?'

'He's not a creep.'

'It's your birthday. Where is he?'

Bella shed her battered cerise suede fringed jacket and crossed her legs below the feathered hem of her minuscule new chiffon skirt, covertly attempting to stretch it to a more reasonable length. Liz had bought the skirt for her birthday. It was far too short but she had to be seen to wear it at least this once.

'So what was Griff the Glib's excuse this time?'

'Wow, look at those wheels!' Bella exclaimed hurriedly, keen for a change of subject. She craned her neck to gaze out at the gleaming silver sports car drawing up outside the five-star hotel on the other side of the street. 'That's a Bugatti Supersport.'

'A what?' Obediently distracted, Liz peered without a lot of interest and then gasped. 'Look who's getting out of it! Now that is what I call—'

'Fabulous engineering.' Bella was eyeing the sleek lines of the powerful car, not the driver with his smouldering, dark good looks. Bella preferred blonds.

'I haven't heard Rico da Silva described in quite those terms before.'

'Who?'

'If you ever put your nose inside a serious newspaper, you'd recognise him too. He's absolutely gorgeous, isn't he?' Liz looked rapt. 'He's also single and loaded!'

'He has a beautiful set of wheels. Is he into motors?'

'He's an international financier. The local paper did a profile on him,' Liz told her. 'He owns a fabulous country estate just outside town. He spent millions renovating it.'

Bella grimaced. Finance...money...banks. She never went into a bank if she could help it, didn't even own a cheque book. People who wheeled and dealed in money and profit made her skin crawl. A faceless smoothie from a bank had pushed Gramps' business to the wall and put him into a premature grave.

'That's his current lady,' Liz murmured as a beautiful blonde woman swathed in fur emerged from the hotel.

Tall, dark and handsome with the little woman. Bella wasn't in the mood to be generous. They looked like some impossibly perfect couple from a glossy magazine. His and hers matching glamour. They had that aura of untouchability which only the seriously rich exuded. It was there like a glass wall between them and the rest of the human race. A clump of pedestrians stopped to let them pass in a direct path to the Bugatti. They took it as their due.

'How the other half lives,' Liz sighed with unhidden envy.

'Time we got this party off the ground!' Bella stood up, spread a brilliantly bright smile round her assembled friends, and switched into extrovert mode.

Dammit, where was the turn-off? Bella called herself a fool for not staying the night with Liz as she had originally planned, but Liz had been in the mood to preach and Bella hadn't been in the mood to listen. Now it was three in the morning. The roads were deserted. And somehow she had got lost. *There* it was! Jumping on the brakes, Bella swung into a frantic last-minute turn. As she made it a gigantic yawn engulfed her taut facial muscles. As she emerged from it, rubbing at her sleepy eyes, another car appeared directly in the path of her headlights.

With a shriek of horror Bella barely had time to brace herself before impact. The jolt of the crash shuddered through her entire body, the sickening noise of buckling metal almost deafening her. Then there was a terrible silence. Fast to react, Bella's first thought was for the other driver. Her windscreen was smashed. She couldn't see a thing. She lurched out of the Skoda on legs that felt like jellied eels.

A hand clamped round her slim shoulder. 'Are you hurt? Have you passengers?'

'No!' Taken aback by someone with even faster reactions than her own, Bella hovered in the biting wind tunnelling down the street as the powerful head and shoulders ducked into the cluttered interior of her car, which more closely resembled a travelling dustbin than a vehicle. Her teeth chattered with shock, her aghast attention logged onto the truly appalling amount of damage done to her car. The whole bonnet was wrecked.

'You madman!' she burst out helplessly. 'What were you doing on the wrong side of the road?'

The large presence straightened. Bella was not small and she was wearing very high heels, but the male beside her still towered above her. In the streetlight his hard, dark features were as unyielding as hewn granite.

'What was I doing?' he repeated in a raw tone of disbelief, and this time she caught the foreign inflexion, the thickness of an accent that was certainly not British.

'Did you forget we drive on the left here?' Bella asked furiously.

'You stupid bitch...you're on a one-way street!' With that he strode back to his own car.

A one-way street? About to open her mouth and loudly disclaim that ridiculous assertion at the same time as she asked him who the hell he thought he was calling a stupid bitch, Bella looked back to the corner and saw the sign. A one-way street. She had turned right into a one-way street and not unnaturally had had a head-on collision. Devastated by the realisation that the accident was entirely her fault, Bella leant against the wing of the Skoda because her knees were threatening to give way.

The other driver was lifting something out of his car. Oh, dear God, what had she hit? For the first time she looked at the other vehicle. It had a hideous *déjà vu* familiarity, only it had looked considerably more pristine earlier. A Bugatti. She had wrecked a Bugatti Supersport which retailed at somewhere around a quarter of a million pounds. She wanted to throw herself down on the road and scream like a banshee in torment. Her insurance premium would rocket into outer space after this... correction; she'd be lucky to *get* insurance. This wasn't her first accident, although it was certainly by far the worst. Dammit, what was the guy's name? Why, oh, why had she let her temper rip and called him a madman?

'What are you doing?' she demanded in a weak voice, moving forward.

He was lounging against his status-symbol car, which was not quite the status symbol it had been. And he had a mobile phone in his hand. Just her luck—a guy with a phone in his car!

'I am calling the police,' he imparted, with a decided edge of, And aren't you going to enjoy that? in his growling delivery.

'The p-police?' Bella stammered shrilly, plunged into further depths of unhidden horror. She turned as white as a sheet.

'Naturally. Why don't you get back into your vehicle and await their arrival?'

'Do we need the police?' she asked in a shaky voice, her heart sinking to the soles of her feet at the prospect of being arrested on a charge of careless driving.

'Of course we need the police.'

Bella took another desperate step forward. 'Please don't get the police!' she muttered frantically.

'I should imagine that you will be breathalysed.'

'I haven't been drinking. I just don't see the necessity to get the police!'

'I expect they already have more than a passing acquaintance with you.' Rico da Silva sent a glittering look of derision over her.

'Well, we wouldn't be complete strangers, let's put it
that way,' Bella conceded, thinking back miserably to
her earliest memories of what her travelling mother had
called police harassment. No matter how hard she tried
Bella had never lost that childhood terror of the uni-
formed men who had moved them on from their illegal
camping grounds.

'I didn't think so. It's a hard life on the street,' he
murmured, shooting her scantily clad, shivering figure
an intent but unreadable glance. 'Heading home from
the nightshift?'

What the hell was he talking about? Struggling to
concentrate, she moved even closer. 'We could sort this
out...just you and me, off the record,' she assured him
in desperation, skimming an anxious glance across the
street as another car passed by, slackened speed to have
a good look at the wreckage, and then drove on. Any
minute now a patrol car would be along.

'*Es verdad*?' Diamond-bright dark eyes scanned her
beautiful, pleading face, his strong jaw line clenching
hard as a long finger stabbed buttons on the mobile
phone without her even being aware of it. 'I don't think
so. In that one field alone I prefer amateurs.'

'Amateur what?' Bella returned in despair, deciding
that *he* had definitely been drinking.

And then she heard the police answering the call,
registered that he had already dialled, and allowed sheer
panic to take over. Snaking out a hand, she grabbed at
the phone. Lean fingers as compelling as steel cuffs
closed round her wrist and jerked it ruthlessly down.
She burst into floods of tears, her overtaxed emotions
shooting to a typically explosive Bella climax and spilling
over instantaneously.

'You bully!' she sobbed accusingly.

With a raw gasp of male fury, the background of the
police telephonist's voice was abruptly silenced as if the

man before her had cut the connection. 'You attacked me!' he grated.

'I just didn't want you to ring the police!' she slung back, on the brink of another howl. 'But go ahead! Have me arrested! I don't care; I'm past caring!'

'Stop making such a noise,' he growled. 'You're making an exhibition of yourself!'

'If I want to have hysterics, that's my business!' she asserted through her tears. 'What do you think *this* is going to do to my insurance?'

There was a short silence.

'You *have* insurance?'

'Of course I have insurance,' Bella mumbled, making an effort to collect herself and keeping a careful distance from him, since he had already proved that he was the aggressive type.

'Give me the details and sign a statement admitting fault and you can be on your way,' he drawled with unhidden relish.

Bella shot him an astonished glance. 'You mean it?'

'*Sí* . . . five more minutes in your company and I will understand why men murder. Not only that, I will be at the forefront of a campaign to bring in the death penalty for women drivers!' Rico da Silva intoned between clenched teeth.

Sexist pig. Smearing her non-waterproof mascara over her cheeks as she wiped at her wet face, Bella bit back the temptation to answer in kind. After all, he was going to be civilised. If he had smashed up *her* Bugatti she probably would have wanted blood too. Prepared to be generous, she still, however, gave a deliberate little rub to her wrist just to let him know that he might not have drawn blood but he might have inflicted bruises.

He planted a sheet of paper on the bonnet and handed her a pen.

'You write it; I'll sign it,' she proffered glumly.

'I want it to be in your handwriting.'

But he still stood over her and dictated what he wanted her to write. She struggled with the big words he used, her rather basic spelling powers taxed beyond their limits.

'This is illiterate,' he remarked in a strained voice.

Bella's cheeks flamed scarlet. Her itinerant childhood had meant that she had very rarely attended a school. Gramps had changed all that when she had gone to live with him but somehow her spelling had never quite come up to scratch. Laziness and lack of interest, she conceded inwardly, for she possessed a formidable intelligence which she focused solely on the field of art. Spelling came a very poor second.

'But it's fine,' Rico da Silva added abruptly, suddenly folding it and stuffing it into the pocket of his dinner jacket.

Seeing him reach for his phone again, she gabbled the name of her insurance company in a rush.

'I'm ringing for a tow-truck for the cars,' he murmured, reading the reanimated fear on her expressive face.

'Oh... Thanks,' she muttered, turning her head and strolling away while he made the call, far more concerned with what it would cost to pay for the towing service. 'I'm sorry about your car. It was beautiful,' she sighed when he had stopped speaking.

'I'll call a cab for you.'

Bella bit out a rueful laugh. She lived in London, which was almost sixty miles away. The cab fare home would be a week's wages—maybe more. 'Forget it.'

'I will pay for it.'

She dealt him a disbelieving look. 'No way.'

'I insist.' He was digging a wallet out of his pocket with astonishing alacrity.

'I said no,' she reminded him flatly, embarrassed to death by the offer and hurriedly attempting to change the subject. 'Cold for May, isn't it?'

'Take the money!' he bit out with stinging impatience.

Bella frowned, hunching deeper into her battered jacket, one long, shapely thigh crossed over the other, her fantastic head of hair blowing back from her exotic features in the breeze. 'What's the matter with you? I have to wait for the tow-truck.'

'I'll wait for it,' he told her harshly.

'Look, it isn't my car...'

'What?' he raked at her.

'It belongs to this old man I live with. I only have the use of it,' Bella explained soothingly.

Narrowed dark eyes rested on her, his beautifully shaped mouth hardening, and she found herself staring at him, noticing the shape of his lips. It was the artist in her, she supposed abstractedly. He would be an interesting study to paint.

'How old is old?' Rico da Silva enquired, surprising her.

'As old as you feel.' Bella laughed in more like her usual manner. 'Hector says he feels fifty on a good day, seventy on a bad. I reckon he's about the latter.'

'And what are you?'

'Twenty-one...' she checked her watch '...and four and a half hours.'

'Yesterday was your birthday?'

'Lousy birthday,' she muttered, more to herself than him. 'I had to work.'

'It happens,' he said in a strained voice.

'And my boyfriend is two-timing me.' It just came out. She hadn't meant to say it. Maybe it was the effect of bravely smiling all evening and keeping her mouth shut with her friends.

'The pensioner?' He sounded even more strained.

It was the language barrier, she decided. How on earth could he imagine that she was dating a man old enough to be her grandfather?

'Not Hector—my boyfriend.'

'Maybe you should think of another occupation— something that keeps you home at night...although perhaps not,' he muttered half under his breath.

Had she told him that she was a waitress? She didn't remember doing so but she must have done. Screening another sleepy yawn, Bella sighed. 'I don't mind most of the time, although it's murder on my feet and it's very boring. Still, it pays the rent—'

'He charges you rent?'

'Of course he does...although not very much.' She yawned again, politely masking her mouth with a slender hand. 'He tried to claim for me as a housekeeper but the Inland Revenue weren't impressed. I'm not really very domestic but he wouldn't like it if I was. It's kind of hard to explain Hector to people...'.

'Are you in the habit of telling complete strangers the most intimate details of your life?' Rico da Silva prompted in a tone of driven fascination.

Bella thought about it and then nodded, although she would have disputed his concept of 'intimate details'. Friends said, 'I told you so.' Strangers just listened and volunteered their own experiences. Not that the male standing next to her would. He was the secretive type, she decided. Still waters ran deep—dark and deep as hell with this one, she thought helplessly.

'You're a financier,' she remarked conversationally, thinking that what was good enough for the gander was good enough for the goose.

'How the hell do you know that?' he shot at her forbiddingly.

Bella gave him a startled look. 'I saw you earlier this evening and a friend told me who you were.'

'And then all of a sudden you crash into me. Two such coincidences in one night strain my credulity!' Rico da Silva shot at her.

'Pretty lousy luck, huh? If I'd done the cards this morning I probably wouldn't have got out of bed—'

'"The cards"?' he echoed.

'Tarot cards. Though mostly I steer clear of the temptation to tell my own fortune these days. Sometimes I think you're better not knowing what's ahead of you.'

'I do not believe in such a coincidence,' he stated afresh, staring down at her in a very intimidating fashion. 'It was your intent to meet me, *es verdad*?'

'You're a very uptight personality.' Bella shook her vibrant head. 'And a bit weird, to be frank—'

'*Weird*?' Rico da Silva roared. 'You think that I am weird?'

She raised her hands. 'Now just count to ten and back off, buster.'

'"Buster"?' he repeated, snatching in a hissing breath.

'Mr Silver...no, it wasn't that, was it?' She sighed.

'Rico...da...Silva,' he enunciated very slowly and carefully, as if he were talking to a complete idiot.

'Yeah, I knew it was something strange. I hate to tell you this but it *is* a little weird to imagine that a total stranger would crash into you *deliberately* to meet you,' Bella told him gently. 'I mean, I might have been killed.'

From beneath black lashes so long that they cast crescent shadows on his savage cheekbones, he cast her a glimmering glance. 'I have known women to take tremendous risks to make my acquaintance.'

'I wonder why?' she said, and then realised by the sudden, thundering silence that she had said it out loud instead of just thinking it. 'What I mean is...well, there's only one way of saying this, Mr da Silver—'

'Silva!' he slotted in rawly.

Uptight wasn't the word for it. This guy lived on the outer edge. On the brink of gently assuring him that he had met some very peculiar women, Bella was silenced briefly by the sight of the tow-truck surging up the street towards them.

'Talk about service!' she gasped. 'I thought we'd be here for hours!'

'Another half-hour of your relentless, mindless chatter and I would be—'

'More hyper than you already are? It's OK. I'm not offended,' she told him with a smile. 'You either love me or you hate me. But, for your own sake, get your blood pressure checked and take up something relaxing like gardening. Guys like you drop dead from heart attacks at forty-five.' Dragging her attention from the darkening colour of his cheekbones and the razor-slash effect of his incredulous gaze, Bella turned to gape at the arrival of a second tow-truck. 'Gosh...one each!'

With that, she rushed over to the Skoda, belatedly realising that she would need to clear the car out. She was kneeling on the driver's seat, poking around amongst the rubbish for stray items of clothing, letters, bills, her sketch-pad and pencils, when his voice assailed her again from behind.

'I will expect you to pass on your insurance details to my secretary tomorrow. This is the number.'

Awkwardly she twisted round and reached out to grasp a gilded card and dig it into her pocket.

'If you don't call, I will inform the police—'

'Look, what are you trying to do—give me nightmares?' she exclaimed helplessly, clinging perilously to the steering wheel to lean out and look up at him. 'I am a law-abiding person.'

'To trust you goes against my every principle,' he admitted unapologetically.

'You wouldn't want me to lose my licence, would you?' Bella fixed enormous green eyes on him in reproach. 'It took me a lot of years to get that licence. The examiners used to draw lots for me and the one that got the short straw was *it*! I mean, we all have weaknesses and mine is in the driving department, but this is truly the very worst accident I have ever had and I am going to be much more careful in the future...cross my heart and hope to die—'

'Or shut up.'

'I beg your pardon?' She squinted up at him.

He extended his phone with an air of long-suffering hauteur. 'Ring your boyfriend to come and pick you up.'

'You've got to be kidding. He'd probably say his car had a flat tyre or something anyway,' she mused, returning to her frantic clean-up.

'There must be somebody you can contact!'

'At four in the morning to take me back to London?' And pigs might fly, her tone said.

'I am not giving you a lift!' he snapped in a whiplash response.

So he had been heading for London too. 'I wasn't aware I asked for one,' she hissed. 'Now why don't you just go away and leave me alone?'

'I am being foolish. No doubt you are accustomed to walking lonely streets at this hour of the night, *es verdad*? But it is hard for me to forget my natural instinct to behave as a gentleman—'

'I would have said you forgot it the minute I hit your car...but it's OK,' Bella continued sweetly. 'I didn't notice. I haven't got much experience of what you would probably call gentlemen. I cut my teeth on creeps.'

There was a fulminating silence.

'Make sure you make that call tomorrow.'

Bella scrambled out backwards with her bulging carrier bag, wondering why he was still hovering. Approaching the driver of the tow-truck, she told him to be sure to dump the Skoda at the *nearest* garage possible. Hopefully that would cut the cost. 'I can't pay you now,' she then said awkwardly. 'I haven't got enough money on me.'

'I will take care of it,' Rico da Silva announced glacially from behind her.

She grimaced and ignored him to ask the driver what it was going to cost. Her horror was unfeigned. 'I'm not asking you to *fix* it!' she protested in a shattered voice.

'I said I will pay the bill!' Rico da Silva blitzed.

Her temples were pounding like crazy. She just couldn't fight any more. Once again she nodded. Anything for a quiet life. She started to walk away. Her feet were killing her.

'Where are you going?'

'The bus station.' She glanced back at him with a frown of incomprehension, well aware that he liked her just about as much as she liked him, wondering why on earth it should matter to him how she intended to get home.

'*Madre de Dios*!' he ground out, skimming a furious hand of frustration through the air. 'There will be no buses until morning!'

'Morning's only a couple of hours away.'

'I'll give you a lift,' he bit out between clenched teeth.

'Forget it.'

'I said I will give you a lift, but only on one condition—you do not open your mouth!'

'I prefer the bus. It's more egalitarian. I'm allowed to breathe, you know, that sort of life-enhancing stuff called oxygen? I use up a lot of it, but thanks all the same.' And then she saw the limousine waiting by the kerb on the other side of the street and her sleepy green eyes widened to their fullest extent. She had assumed that he was catching a cab. But a lift in a real live limo... She just couldn't resist the offer. 'Mr da Silva?' she called abruptly.

'I thought you might change your mind,' he breathed, without turning his glossy dark head. 'I must be out of my mind to be doing this.'

'Doing what?'

'Give my chauffeur your address and then shut up,' he grated.

Bella climbed in and surveyed the opulent interior with unhidden fascination. 'Do you always travel... sorry, I forgot!'

The limo purred away from the kerb. Her companion stabbed a button, and under the onslaught of her incredulous scrutiny a revolving drinks cabinet smoothly appeared. 'Wow,' she said, deeply impressed.

'Do you want a drink?' he asked shortly.

'No, thanks. My father was next door to being an alcoholic. Personally speaking, I wouldn't touch the stuff with a barge-pole!'

He expelled his breath in a hiss. She watched his hand still and then hover momentarily before he finally grasped the whisky bottle.

'I guess—'she began, and then sealed her mouth again as those black-as-night eyes hit on her with silencing effect.

'You guess what?' he finally gritted. 'Don't keep me in suspense!'

'I was going to say that we don't have a lot in common, do we? It's a bit like meeting an alien,' Bella mumbled, sleep catching up on her as she rested her heavy head back against the leather upholstery and closed her drooping eyelids. 'Except even the alien might have had a sense of humour...'

Someone was shaking her shoulder hard. She surfaced groggily, registered that she was lying face down on some kind of seat, then remembered and hauled herself upright into a sitting position.

'This cannot be where you live!' Rico da Silva vented with raw exasperation. 'Is this your idea of a joke?'

Bella focused on the familiar Georgian square of enormous, elegant terraced houses, which had been her home for the past year. 'Why should it be my idea of a joke?' She fumbled with the door-release mechanism but the door remained stubbornly closed.

'I should imagine that not one in a thousand hookers lives in a house worth millions!'

'Hookers'? He thought she was a hooker? He thought
she sold her body for money? Aghast, Bella stared at
him for several seemingly endless seconds, telling herself
that she had somehow misunderstood him. 'You think
I'm a prostitute?' she finally gasped, wide-eyed with
rampant disbelief. 'How *dare* you? Let me out of this
car right now!'

A winged ebony brow quirked. 'Are you saying now
that you are not?'

'Of course I'm not!' Bella threw at him in violent
outrage, belatedly understanding all of his peculiar ut-
terances. 'I've never been so insulted in my life! You
have a mind like a sewer—'

'You dress like one—'

'*Dress* like one?' Liz's wretched too short skirt! She
wanted to scream.

'And you came on to me like a whore!' he condemned, without batting an eyelash.

'"Came on to" you?' Fit to be tied, Bella looked at
him with splintering green eyes. '*Me*...come on to you?
Are you crazy?'

'You offered yourself to me—'

'I *what*? You're a lunatic... Let me out of this car;
I don't feel safe!' she shrieked. 'I should never have got
into it in the first place. I knew you were weird!'

'Are you trying to tell me that I was mistaken?' His
strong, dark features were fiercely clenched.

'How dare you think I would come on to you?' Bella
spat at him like a bristling cat. 'I never go for dark men!
Your car was at more risk than you were! And I may
wear second-hand clothes, talk with an Essex accent and
hardly be able to spell, but that doesn't mean that I don't
have principles! It might interest you to know that I'm
a virgin—'

He burst into spontaneous laughter. In fact he threw
his dark head back and very nearly choked on his disbelief. Bella launched herself across the car at him in a

rage and two strong hands snaked out and closed round
her narrow forearms to hold her imprisoned mere inches
from him and in devastating contact with every line of
his leashed, powerful body.

'A virgin?' he queried in a shaking voice. 'Maybe not
a whore... but definitely not a virgin.'

'Let go of me!'

For a split-second he stared down into her brilliant
green eyes and something happened inside her—something that had never happened to Bella before; a tight
clenched sensation jerked low in her stomach. It made
the hair prickle at the back of her neck, the breath catch
in her throat, every muscle draw taut. She looked back
at him with dawning comprehension and horror, feeling
the swell of her own breasts, the sudden, painful tightening of her nipples.

'So what *do* you do on the nightshift?' Rico da Silva
probed in a purring undertone that set up a strange chain
reaction down her spine.

Seriously shaken by the reaction of her own treacherous body, she remained mutinously silent.

'And where *does* Hector fit in?'

'Let go of me... I don't feel well,' Bella muttered
tremulously, and it was true.

He searched her pallor, abruptly freeing her. His ebony
brows had drawn together in a sudden frown. She had
the strangest feeling that he was as disconcerted by his
own behaviour as she had been.

'I'll talk to your secretary tomorrow,' she mumbled,
her nerves strung so tightly that tension was a fevered
pulse-beat through her entire body.

He pressed a button. The chauffeur climbed out and
opened the door in the humming silence. Bella flew out
like a cork ejected from a bottle and fled up the steps
of the shabbiest house in the row. Inserting her key, she
unlocked the front door, then rushed into the shelter of
the dark house and rested back against the door like

someone who had seen death at close quarters. Every
sense on super-alert, she listened to the limo driving off
before she breathed again.

Shock was still reverberating through her. She had felt
so safe for so long. *That* had never happened to her
before with a man. And then all of a sudden, when it
was least expected, she had been gripped by the most
dangerous drive in the entire human repertoire—sexual
desire. But she was really proud of herself. Control and
common sense had triumphed. She had run like a rabbit.

CHAPTER TWO

IN THE half-light Bella picked her way past the piled-up books and newspapers that littered every stair and headed up to the second floor and the privacy of her spacious, cluttered studio. She was still shaking like a leaf. So *that* was what it felt like! She lit the candle beside her bed, and slowly drew in a deep, sustaining breath. Well, thankfully she was extremely unlikely ever to see him again. There was no need to worry about temptation in that quarter. Even so, she was still shaken.

'I go with my feelings—that can never be wrong,' Cleo had once said loftily, supremely blind to the wreckage of disastrous relationships in her past. Her mother had been like a kamikaze pilot with men. Every creep within a hundred-mile radius had zeroed in on her, stopped a while and then moved on. But Cleo had kept on trying, regardless of the consequences to herself and her daughter, always convinced that the *next* one would be different. And Liz could have no idea just how much it scared Bella to be told that she suffered from a similar lack of judgement with the men in her life.

When she came downstairs later that morning Hector was shuffling about in his carpet slippers in the ancient kitchen. The gas bill had arrived. He was taking it as hard as he always did when a bill came through the letter box. There were the usual charged enquiries about how often she had used the oven and boiled the kettle. Hector Barsay's mission in life was to save money.

It was his one failing but, as Gramps had often said, everybody had their little idiosyncrasies, and those same little idiosyncrasies got a tighter hold the older you got.

Beneath his crusty, dismal manner Hector was kind. He had a bunch of prosperous relatives just waiting for him to die so that they could sell his house and make their fortunes. None of them had visited since the time they had tried to persuade him into an old folks' home and he had threatened to leave them out of his will.

'I crashed the car last night,' Bella told him tautly.

'Again?' Hector cringed into his shabby layers of woolly cardigans and she squirmed, guilt and shame engulfing her.

'It's not going to cost you anything!' she swore.

'I haven't got anything!' His faded blue eyes rolled in his head at the very suggestion that his pocket might be touched.

'That's what you have insurance for,' she told him in consolation. 'Before you know it the Skoda will be back in the garage as good as new.'

Back upstairs, she dug out her insurance details and wrinkled her nose. The renewal hadn't yet been sent but then they always took their time about that and, to be fair, she had been a little late in sending on the money because Hector had made her ring round half of London trying to get a cheaper quote. When you had to do it from a phone box, that took time.

She headed out for a phone. Hector insisted that his phone was only to be used in an emergency. The girl at the insurance company was chatty until Bella explained about the accident. Then she went off the line for a while.

'I'm sorry, Miss Jennings,' she murmured on her return, 'but at the time of the accident you were not insured with us—'

'What are you talking about?' Bella was aghast.

'Your premium should have arrived by Tuesday. Unfortunately it was two days late—'

'But surely—?'

'You were given an adequate period in which to respond to the renewal notice.'

'But I—'

'We will be returning your premium in the post. The offer was not accepted within the stated period and we are entitled to withdraw it.'

Argument got Bella nowhere. Reeling with shock, she stood back to let the next person in the queue use the phone. From her pocket she removed the card that Rico da Silva had given her. How could she ring his secretary and tell her she had no insurance? Dear heaven, that was a criminal offence!

A Bugatti... In anguish she clutched at her hair, her stomach heaving. And what about the repair of Hector's Skoda? She would be in debt for the rest of her life. Maybe she would go to prison! Rico da Silva had that piece of paper on which she admitted turning the wrong way into a one-way street without due care and attention!

An hour later Bella was hanging over a reception desk and smiling her most pleading smile. 'Please... this is a matter of life and death!'

'Mr da Silva's secretary, Miss Ames, has no record of your name, Miss Jennings. You are wasting your time and mine,' the elegant receptionist said frigidly.

'But I've already explained that. He probably forgot about it, you know? He had a late night!' Bella appealed in despair.

'If you don't remove yourself from this desk I will be forced to call security.'

'At four this morning Rico told me to ring his secretary!' Bella exclaimed, shooting her last bolt.

Sudden silence fell in the busy foyer. Heads turned. The receptionist's eyes widened and were swiftly concealed by her lashes, faint colour burnishing her cheeks. 'Excuse me for a moment,' she said in a stilted voice.

Bella chewed anxiously at her lower lip and watched her retreat to the phone again; only, this time the conversation that took place was very low-key. She skimmed a hand down over her slim black Lycra skirt, adjusted her thin cotton fitted jacket and surveyed the scuffed toes of her fringed cowboy boots. A clump of suited men nearby were studying her as if she had just jumped naked out of a birthday cake.

But then it was that kind of building—a bank. Just being inside it gave her the heebie-jeebies. All marble pillars and polished floors and hushed voices. Sort of like a funeral parlour, she reflected miserably. And she didn't belong here. She remembered that time she had gone to plead Gramps' case and the executive had been so smooth and nice that she had thought she was actually getting somewhere. But double-talk had been created for places like this. The bank had still called in the debt and Gramps had lost everything.

'Miss Ames will see you,' the receptionist whispered out of the corner of her mouth. 'Take that lift in the corner.'

'How can I help you, Miss Jennings?' She was greeted by the svelte older woman as the lift doors opened on the top floor.

'I need to see Mr da Silva urgently.'

'I'm afraid that Mr da Silva is in a very important meeting and cannot be disturbed. Perhaps you would like to leave a message?'

'I'll wait.' Bella groaned. 'Maybe you could send a message in to him?'

'And what would you like this message to say?'

'Can I come in...like, go and sit down?'

The older woman stepped reluctantly aside.

Loan-sharking certainly paid. Bella took in her palatial surroundings without surprise. 'I'll write the message.'

A notepad was extended to her. Bella dashed off four words, ripped off the sheet, folded it five times into a tiny scrap and handed it over.

'Mr da Silva does not like to be disturbed.'

'He's going to like what I have to tell him even less,' Bella muttered, sprawling down on a sofa.

Miss Ames disappeared. The brunette at the desk watched her covertly as though she was afraid that she was about to pocket the crystal ashtray on the coffee-table. Two minutes later Miss Ames returned, all flushed and taut.

'Come this way, please...'

Bella strode up the corridor, hands stuck in her pockets, fingers curled round the pack of cigarettes that nerves had driven her to buy before she'd entered the bank.

'What the hell are you doing here?' Rico da Silva blazed across the width of the most enormous office she had ever seen. Her heels were sinking into the carpet.

She looked around her with unhidden curiosity and then back at him. He had to be about six feet four. Wide shoulders, narrow hips, long, lean legs. Michelangelo's *David* trapped in the clothing chains of convention. Navy pinstriped suit, boring white shirt, predictable navy tie—he probably put on a red one for Christmas and thought he was being really daring. He was looking her over as if she were a computer virus threatening to foul up the entire office network. She tilted her chin, and her gaze collided with glittering golden eyes...

He had really gorgeous eyes. In the streetlight she hadn't got the full effect. Eyes the colour of the setting sun, spectacularly noticeable in that hard-angled, bronzed face. Eyes that sizzled and burned. The key to the soul. There was a tiger in there fighting to get free—a sexual tiger, all teeth and claws and passion. On some primal level she could feel the unholy heat. Wow, this guy *wants* me, she registered in serious shock.

'I asked you what the hell you're doing here,' Rico repeated with leashed menace.

Bella dragged her distracted gaze from his, astonished to discover how hard it was to break that connection.

Reddening, she went tense all over, embarrassed by her last crazy thought. 'I said it in my note.'

'And what exactly is "*We* have a problem" intended to denote? By the way, problem is spelt with an e, not an a,' he delivered, hitting her on her weakest flank.

'I'll try to remember that.' She studied her feet and then abruptly, cravenly yielded to temptation and dug out the cigarettes and matches. Never had she been more in need of the crutch she had abandoned the day she'd moved into Hector's house. She was just on the brink of lighting up when both the match and cigarette were snatched from her. Under her arrested gaze the cigarette was snapped in two and dropped in a waste-paper basket.

'A member of the hang-'em-high anti-smoking Reich?' Bella probed helplessly.

'What do you think?'

She felt that she had never needed a cigarette more. 'Just one...?' she begged.

'Don't be pathetic. It won't cut any ice with me,' he drawled, with a sardonic twist to his mouth. 'What is the problem?'

Bella swallowed hard and then breathed in deeply.

'You look guilty as sin,' Rico informed her grimly. 'And if my suspicions as to what has prompted this personal appearance prove correct I'm taking you straight to the police.'

The tip of her tongue slid out to moisten her dry lower lip. His lashes lowered. Hooded eyes, revealing a mere slit of gold, dropped to her mouth and lingered there. A buzzing tension entered the atmosphere. The silence vibrated.

As Bella laid her outdated insurance policy on the desk in front of him she felt as though she was moving in slow motion. 'Can I sit down?'

'May I sit down,' he corrected automatically. 'No.'

He scanned the document.

'You see, it only ran out Monday,' Bella pointed out, in a wobbly plea for understanding. 'And I sent in the new premium and thought it was fine. But when I phoned the company this morning...'

The well-shaped, dark head lifted. Lancing golden eyes bit into her shrinking flesh. 'You were driving without insurance when you hit me—'

'Not intentionally!' Bella gasped, raising both hands, palms outward, in a gesture of sincerity. 'I had no idea. I thought I was covered. I'd sent off the money and I bet that if I hadn't had an accident they would have just accepted it and renewed my insur—'

'You're whining,' Rico cut in icily as he rose from behind his impressive desk.

'I'm not whining. I'm only trying to explain!' she protested.

'Point one—if you were not covered by insurance at the time of the accident the oversight was your responsibility. Yours, nobody else's,' he stressed with a glacial lack of compassion. 'Point two—in driving a car without insurance you were committing an offence—'

'But—'

'And point three—I most unwisely chose to let you go scot-free from the consequences of the offence you had *already* committed last night!'

'What offence...? Oh, the one-way street bit,' Bella muttered, hunching her narrow shoulders in self-defence. It was like being under physical attack. 'But that was an accident... It's not as though it was deliberate. Anyone can have an accident, can't they? I'm really sorry. I mean, I would do just about anything for it not to have happened, because now everything's in this horrible mess—'

'For you, not for me.' Rico sent her a hard, impassive look. 'When I inform my insurance company of this they will insist that I bring in the police and they will pursue you for the outstanding monies in a civil case.'

Bella went white and twisted her hands, moving from one long, shapely leg on to the other with stork-like restiveness. 'Please don't get the police. Somehow I'll pay you back...I promise!' she swore unsteadily.

'Is Hector going to pay?'

Bella flinched. 'No,' she mumbled.

'I've already had a quote for the damage to my car.' He gave it to her. Bella watched the carpet tilt and rise as she fought off a sick attack of dizziness brought on by shock. 'Somehow I don't think that you can come up with that kind of cash.'

'Only in instalments.' And if I starved, lived rough and went naked, she added mentally, beginning to tremble. He had spelt out the cold, hard facts and her vague idea that they might somehow be able to come to an arrangement had bitten the dust fast. She couldn't expect him to pay for the repairs to the Bugatti and wait for twenty years for her to settle the debt. Intelligence told her that, but a numbing sense of terror was spreading through her by the second.

'Not acceptable. So therefore it goes through *on* the record with the police,' Rico da Silva informed her flatly.

Already she was backing away, knowing that she was about to break her most unbreakable rule and copy Cleo. She was going to run, pack a bag and leave London— go back to the old life where there were no names, no pack drill, little chance of being caught by the authorities. How had she ever got the idea that she could make it in this other world with all its rules and regulations?

'You're not leaving,' he warned her grimly.

'You can't keep me h-here!' Bella stammered fearfully. 'You can put the police on to me but you can't keep me here!'

'I call Security or I call the police. I'm not a fool. If you walk out of here you'll disappear. Maybe the police are already looking for you,' Rico da Silva suggested, studying her slender, quivering, white-faced figure with cool assessment. 'For some other offence?'

'I don't know what you're talking about!'

'You're terrified.' His shrewd gaze rested intently on her. 'A bit over the top for a charge of careless driving and doing so without insurance. If it's a first offence you'll be fined. However, if this is merely the latest in a line of other misdemeanours I can quite see why you wouldn't want the police brought in.'

In his mind she had already gone from being a lousy driver to being a persistent offender. She had met prejudice like that before. Her first year with Gramps had been hell outside the sanctuary of his home. Neighbours, teachers and classmates had been all too ready to point the finger at Bella when there had been a spate of thieving in school. Bella had never stolen anything in her life, but had the true culprit not been caught in the act she was well aware that everyone would have continued to believe her guilty.

With the last ounce of her pride she thrust her head high. 'I have a clean record!'

'*Excelente*. Then you will not throw a fit of hysterics when I take you to the police station.'

'*You* . . . take me to the p-police station?' The fire in her was doused, cold fear taking over.

'Tell me why you are so petrified of the police,' he invited, almost conversationally.

'None of your bloody business!'

His strikingly handsome features clenched. 'It's not my problem. I suggest we get this over with. I have a busy day ahead of me.'

'I'm not going to any police station with you!' Bella gasped strickenly. 'You'd have to knock me out and drag me by the hair!'

'Don't tempt me.' Rico da Silva sent a look of pure derision raking over her, his eloquent mouth compressing. 'And stop play-acting. I'm not impressed.

You're no shrinking violet, *querida*. What you've got
you flaunt!'

'Don't talk to me like that!'

'I took pity on you last night, but when you strolled
in here today you made a very big mistake,' he asserted
with cold emphasis. 'You thought all you had to do was
flash those fabulous legs and the rest of that devastating
body and I'd be willing to…shall we say…negotiate?'

'I didn't think that!' Bella objected in sick disbelief.

'*Si*…yes, you did.' Rico vented a harsh laugh that
chilled her. '*Dios mío*…you may not be able to spell
anything above two syllables but you market flesh like
a real professional. Hot and cold. I could have had you
last night if I had wanted you. And I did want you. Just
for a moment. There isn't a man in this building who
wouldn't want you… You're an exceptionally beautiful
young woman,' he conceded very drily. 'But I don't play
around with whores. I never have and I never will.'

She was shattered by his view of her, could not begin
to understand what she had done to arouse such brutal
hostility. Nausea stirred in her stomach. She felt soiled.
Apart from that final moment inside his limousine last
night she had been totally unaware of him as a *man*,
even as a very attractive man. She had made no attempt
to attract him. She hadn't flirted or looked or done anything which could have warranted this attack on her.

Yet now he was calling her a whore again, clearly still
convinced that she was at the very least promiscuous
and the kind of woman who used her body like a bar-
gaining counter in a tight corner. It was an image so far
removed from reality that she told herself she should be
laughing. But instead it hurt—it hurt like a knife inside
her breast just the way it had hurt when the village had
whispered about her behind her back all those years ago.

He closed a firm hand round her arm and propelled
her out of his office towards the lift. Her dazed eyes
caught the amazement on his secretary's face as she ap-

peared in a doorway. Bella was too shocked to relocate her tongue before they were inside the lift.

'You're out of your mind,' she whispered, her temples thumping with tension.

'Tell it to the police.'

'You're not t-taking me to the police!' Panic set in again as she was recalled to the reality of his intentions. Like an animal suddenly finding herself in a trap, she whirled round, hands flailing against the stainless-steel walls as she sought escape.

He grabbed her with strong hands and settled her back against the wall.

'Let go of me!' she screamed, without warning running violently out of control. Fear was splintering through her in blinding waves. 'Let me go, you bastard!'

He pinned her carefully still with the superior weight and strength of his hard-muscled length. He spat something at her in Spanish, glaring down at her with incandescent eyes of gold and blatant incomprehension. 'I'm not going to hurt you. Why are you behaving like this? Calm down,' he bit out from between even white teeth.

'Let me go... *Let me go!*' she chanted wildly. '*Please!*'

'If I don't take you to the police I'll take you home.' Every muscle in his dark features rigid, he slung her a look of smouldering sexual appraisal which was flagrant enough to make her knees sag and her darkened eyes fill with an ocean of sheer shock. '*Sí*... and bed you like you've never been bedded before! I have never wanted anything as badly as I want you, and the knowledge that I can afford you doesn't help. It's a sick craving and I am not yielding to it,' he muttered roughly, so close now that she could feel his breath on her cheek as his dark head lowered, degree by mesmerising degree. 'And, if I did, you'd be sorry. Believe me, the police are the *soft* option...'

His voice seemed to be coming from miles away. There were so many other things stealing her attention—the

heat of his body and the warm, oddly familiar scent of
him, the pounding in her veins and the race of her
heartbeat, the hot, tight, excitement clutching at her.
These were sensations so new and so powerful that they
imprisoned her.

His mouth crashed down on hers. Electric shock
sizzled through every skin cell. Nothing that intense had
ever happened to her before. His tongue stabbed between her lips and heat surged between her thighs. She
quivered, letting him splay his hands intimately to the
swell of her hips, lifting her to him, melding every inch
of her screamingly willing body to the hungry threat of
his. It still wasn't close enough to satisfy. A moan escaped huskily from the back of her throat—a curiously
animal moan that she did not recognise as her own.

Abruptly he broke the connection. He broke it with
such force, thrusting her back from him, that momentarily she slumped back against the cold wall, surveying
him with unseeing eyes glazed by confusion. The lift
doors suddenly glided back, letting in a rush of cold air,
bringing her to her senses.

Every instinct Bella had was urging her to run. She
took off through the doors, the blurred images of parked
cars assailing her on all sides. A car park, an under-
ground car park. Two large men were standing just
beyond the lift, both of them moving forward, then
hesitating, twin expressions of stunned incredulity
freezing their faces.

'Get the hell out of here!' Rico da Silva roared at them.

'But Mr da Silva—?'

'*Out*!'

Seconds later Bella's run was concluded. She made it
about halfway down the shadowy aisle of cars before
she was intercepted by a hand hauling her back as if she
were a rag doll. As he spun her round she kicked him
in the shin, and would have kicked him somewhere that
hurt even more if she had had the time to aim better.

'You pervert!' she sobbed with rage.

'You loved it,' he slung at her, grimacing with pain as he hauled her back to him with remorseless determination.

'Don't move... If you don't move, nobody will get hurt,' a completely strange male voice intoned flatly in a startling interruption.

'What the—?' As Rico's head spun round he fell silent, his entire body freezing with a tension that leapt through Bella as well like a lightning bolt.

Following the stilled path of his gaze, Bella looked in turn at the two men standing there. They were wearing black Balaclavas. Both of them had guns. Her jaw dropped, a sharp exhalation of air hissing from her.

'Keep quiet... Now back away from him slowly.' The taller one was addressing her. *Her*! Bella blinked, paralysed to the spot, unable to believe that the men weren't a figment of her imagination, and yet, on some sixth-sense level, accepting them, fearing them, sensing their cold menace. 'Move... What a clever girl you've been, getting rid of his guards, but frankly you're surplus to requirements. Is she worth anything to you?'

The scream just exploded from Bella. She didn't think about screaming, didn't even know it was coming. The noise just whooshed up out of her chest and flew from her strained mouth—a long, primal wail of terror. And the taller man flew at her, knocking her to the ground so hard that he drove the breath from her lungs and bruised every bone in her body. A large hand closed over her mouth and then something pricked her shoulder, making her gasp with pain...and she was plunging down into a frightening, suffocating tunnel of darkness.

CHAPTER THREE

BELLA was cold and sore. Her head was aching. Something was banging. It sounded like metal on metal—a brutal, crashing noise. Maybe it was inside her head. She had a horrible taste in her mouth and her throat hurt. Her arm was throbbing as well. She felt every sensation separately. Her brain was shrouded in a fog of disorientation. Thinking was an unbearable effort, but she willed her eyes to open.

Her dilated, still semi-drugged gaze fell on a blank wall. She moved her head and moaned with discomfort. She was lying on a bed—a hard, narrow bed. The unbearable banging stopped, but her ears were still so full of it that it was a while before she could actually hear. And then she heard footsteps.

'I was hoping you'd stay comatose. Then I wouldn't be tempted to kill you...'

The tangle of glorious hair moved and she turned over. 'Rico?' she said thickly.

'Why didn't I call Security? Why didn't I just ring the police?' Rico da Silva breathed in a driven undertone as he stared furiously down at her. 'Shall I tell you why? I let lust come between me and my wits. *Dios mío* ... the one time in my life I stray off the straight and narrow I land the gypsy's curse and nearly get myself killed. If I come out of this alive I'm still going to take you to that police station! And, if there is any justice in the British legal system, you'll be locked up for ever!'

Her lashes fluttered during this invigorating speech. Then, slowly, jerkily, she pulled herself up onto her knees. 'What happened?' she mumbled weakly.

'I've been kidnapped.'

'Oh.' Incredibly it didn't mean anything to her until she remembered those final few minutes in the car park. The men, the guns, the violence. A wave of sick dizziness assailed her. 'Oh, dear God...' she said shakily.

Rico da Silva already looked so different. His jacket and tie had been discarded. His shirt was smeared with grime. His black hair was astonishingly curly, tousled out of its sleek, smooth style. 'No hysteria!' he warned with lethal brevity.

'You said...*you* have been kidnapped. But I'm here too.' Bella swung her legs down and slid slowly off the bed.

'I begged them to leave you behind. I told them you were so thick that you wouldn't be capable of assisting the police. I told them you were worthless...'

She thought about it. 'Thanks...I suppose you did your best.'

'Do you have a single, living brain cell?' Rico slashed at her without warning. 'Am I condemned to spend what may well be my last hours on this earth with a halfwit?'

Bella stiffened as though she had been struck. She was far from halfwitted. Indeed, she had an IQ rating which put her into the top two per cent of the population, but that was a fact she never shared. It tended either to intimidate or antagonise people.

Rico da Silva wanted an argument, she sensed. She understood that. He needed to hit out and she was the nearest quarry. Forgivingly she ignored him and concentrated on exploring their immediate environment and its peculiarities. She touched the wall. 'It's metal.'

'Be grateful. At least they gave us airholes.'

She wasn't listening. She scanned the bed, the single chair, the lit battery lamp. It was the only source of light. And she was used to the kind of light that came from paraffin, gas and batteries. She had grown up with it, sat in darkness when there was no money for replenishment. There was no window. She brushed past him to pass through the incongruous beaded curtain covering a doorway which his bulk had been obscuring.

In the dim light beyond she saw a gas-powered fridge, a small table, another chair, an old cupboard, and what looked like a tiny, old-fashioned stove heater connected by a flue to the metal roof. And then she glimpsed the door. She grabbed at the handle, suddenly frantic to see daylight, and was denied. The wooden partition concealed only a toilet and a sink. No windows—no windows anywhere. Her throat closed. She rammed down her panic and drew in a sustaining breath.

'What are we in?' she demanded starkly.

'A steel transport container. Most ingenious,' Rico explained without any emotion at all. 'I hope you're not claustrophobic.'

She never had been until now. Automatically she felt the cold metal walls, stood on tiptoe to touch the roof, felt the airholes he had mentioned, and a long, cold shudder of fear took her in its hold. 'It's like a metal tomb.'

'What time is it? My watch was smashed.'

Somehow that casual enquiry helped her to get a grip on herself. Moving back through the curtain into the other section, she peered down at her watch. 'Ten past seven.'

'Time to eat.'

'*Eat*?' Bella echoed shrilly. 'We've just been kidnapped and you want to eat? I want to get out of here!'

'And you think I don't?' Lean fingers gripped her taut shoulders as he yanked her forward. Grim dark eyes held hers. 'I've been conscious for two hours longer than you. I have been over every centimetre of every surface of this metal cell. But for the airholes it's solid steel. We have nothing here capable of cutting through solid steel,' he spelt out with cool, flat emphasis. 'Have you ever looked at the bolts on container doors? That is the only other option...'

She glanced past him to see the doors which were so closely shut that they were almost indistinguishable from the other walls. 'We'll never get through those either,' she mumbled sickly. 'People have died in these containers... suffocated, starved—'

'I have not the slightest intention of suffocating or starving,' Rico cut in with ruthless assurance. 'And, if one is permitted to take hope from appearances, neither have my kidnappers any such intention. Dead, I'm not worth a cent.'

'Ap-pearances?' she prompted jerkily.

'Someone's gone to a lot of trouble to plan this operation and take the minimum number of risks,' Rico pointed out. 'The necessities of life have been supplied. We have food and water. They have no immediate need to venture into further contact with us. They must be very confident we cannot escape. This leads me to believe that for the moment we are as safe as it is possible to be in such a situation.'

'S-safe?'

'I would feel more threatened if one of them was sitting in here with us,' Rico said drily. 'Or someone had come along to tell me to stop making such a racket when I was thumping the walls.'

'The noise—that was you,' she registered, shaking her head.

'I wanted to know if there was a guard out there... or even if it was possible to attract anyone's attention. But, this time, no joy.' His sculpted mouth tightened to a thin, hard line. 'However, we will keep on trying. There is always the chance that we could be heard at any time of the day or night.'

'Yes.' He was giving her something to hang on to—a slender hope. Bella nodded, almost sick with the nerves that were threatening her wavering composure. He had

had the time and privacy supplied by her uncon-
sciousness to come to terms with their situation. She had
not had that time or that privacy. She was angry and
scared to the same degree. Somebody had deprived her
of the most basic of human rights—freedom. But even
worse than that was the terror that in the end they might
take her life as well.

'You hear that silence?' His nostrils flared as he flung
his dark head back. 'Now we listen for some sound of
humanity—traffic, a dog barking... anything.'

'These walls would act like double glazing, I bet. A
friend of mine has just got new windows in and you
can't hear the traffic through them...' Her voice trailed
to a halt as she glimpsed Rico's arrested expression.
'Sorry, I sort of rattle on some—'

'Stop rattling,' he articulated with ruthless precision.
'You mentioned food?'

'In the fridge.'

'Enough for two?' she whispered as it suddenly
dawned on her that his kidnappers could never have
planned on having to imprison two people.

'We'll conserve it as far as possible. The same with
the light. We have no idea how long we will be here,' he
delivered smoothly.

The wild idea that in a strange way Rico da Silva was
in his element occurred to her. It doused her urge to
scream and shout uncontrollably. Pride kept her quiet.
There he was, certainly tense but on the surface as cool
as ice.

'Anybody could be forgiven for thinking that this has
happened to you before!' she muttered with scantily
leashed resentment.

'I have been prepared for this situation by profes-
sionals. Although I admit I did not expect to have to
put what I learnt into action.'

Bella flashed through the beaded curtain and sank
down on the chair by the table. Wrapping her hands

together, she bowed her head. She just could not believe that this was happening to her. She just could not credit that she had been kidnapped. That was something that occurred to strangers in the headlines ... and they didn't all come out alive! Her stomach heaved again.

'How rich are you, Rico?' she asked in a wobbly voice.

'Filthy rich.'

'Good.'

He had said that the kidnapping had been well organised. Hopefully they were not in the hands of maniacs. There would be a ransom demand and Rico's bank or his family or whatever, she thought vaguely, would pay up and they would be released just as soon as the money was handed over.

'Will they want money for me?' she muttered helplessly.

'I doubt it.'

She was worthless. His own assertion to the kidnappers drifted back to her. And she didn't know whether to be glad or sorry. She had been in the wrong place at the wrong time, an innocent bystander caught up in something that was nothing to do with her. And it was *his* fault. But for him she wouldn't have been in that car park! On the other hand, if anything happened to Rico—if, for instance, stress made him drop dead with a coronary—the kidnappers might just kill her to get rid of her. 'Surplus to requirements'... Nobody was going to pay for her release!

'Are you healthy?' she whispered.

'Very.'

In silent relief she nodded. But still she couldn't believe that it was real. Just twenty-four hours ago she had not even known that Rico da Silva walked this earth. Helplessly she pointed out to him that this time yesterday they had not even met.

'And wasn't ignorance bliss?'

'I don't see why you have to be so nasty!' Bella snapped. 'Personally I think I'm taking this very well. I've already been threatened and assaulted by you—'

'By *me*?' A lean hand thrust the beaded strands aside. Poised in the doorway, Rico surveyed her with incredulous, blazing golden eyes. The cool-as-ice impression was only on the surface, she registered. Beneath it lurked a deep well of near-murderous rage, rigorously suppressed and controlled.

'Yes, by you. Then I get thumped and drugged and kidnapped. I wouldn't have been there if it hadn't been for you!' she suddenly spat.

'And I wouldn't be here now if it wasn't for you.'

'I b-beg your pardon?'

Black lashes dropped, screening his piercing gaze. 'Forget I said that—'

'Oh, no, as you once said to me, don't keep me in suspense!' she shrieked.

'Cool down...and grow up,' Rico drawled in a soft tone that none the less stung like acid. 'How we got here is unimportant. The only item on our agenda now is survival.'

Bella studied the floor, tears burning at the back of her eyes. It was shock. She was still in shock. She wanted to ask him what he had meant just now. She wanted to know what had happened after she'd blanked out back in that car park. But she pinned her tremulous lips together instead.

'Let's eat.'

Eager to do something, she leapt off the chair and opened the fridge. It was bunged to the gills. Great, she thought for a split-second. Her next thought was entirely different. Dear God, how long were his kidnappers planning to keep them here? And, assuming that they hadn't added to the hoard when they'd realised that they had not one but two victims requiring sustenance, that was an enormous amount of food...most of which wouldn't keep that long even in a fridge—salad stuffs, cold meats, cheeses, milk, bread, butter. All perishable.

'There is a stock of tinned goods in the cupboard as well as extra lights and several batteries, plates and cutlery.'

'We could light another lamp—'

'We don't need it. Anything that we don't need we save,' he reminded her.

Bella burrowed into the cupboard, locating a tin of stew. 'If you light that stove, I could heat this on that little hotplate.'

'There's no fuel.'

'We could smash up a chair or something,' Bella persisted, shivering.

'The ventilation in here is wholly inadequate. Fumes might not escape. We could be suffocated. The stove cannot be lit.'

The boss man had spoken. Bloody know-it-all! Her teeth ground together. It was freezing cold and it was likely to get considerably colder. He had a lot more clothes on than she had. And where the heck was she to sleep? One bed. Two dining chairs. A metal floor. Guess who would get the floor?

She found a bowl and peeled some leaves off a lettuce, before marching through to the sink which had the sole water supply. When she returned she stood at the cupboard, her back turned to him, washing the salad. And guess who gets to prepare the meal? she thought caustically.

She felt slightly foolish when she turned round to find that he already had two plates on the table, sparsely filled. The pieces of hacked cheese and the tomatoes complete with stalks made her mouth unexpectedly curve up into a grin. He was even less domesticated than she, but she liked him for making the effort.

'What happened after I got the needle in my arm?' she asked flatly as he reappeared with the second chair and she sat down.

An ebony brow quirked. 'Why talk about it?'

'Because *I* want to know!'

'I was afraid you would be shot when you screamed. The smaller one was very nervous. He was taking aim when the other one brought you down.'

Bella bit at her lower lip. 'I didn't mean to scream.'

'I suppose it was a natural response,' Rico conceded shortly, his mouth clenching.

But not a miscalculation that he would have been guilty of making, she gathered. He had been on all systems alert but in icy control. And for some reason he wasn't telling her the whole story. She sensed that. 'What did you do?'

'I deflected his aim,' Rico admitted.

'How?'

'By wrenching his arm.'

Perspiration broke out on her brow at the image which his admission evoked. 'You could have been killed!'

'I could not stand by and do nothing.'

'And then what happened?'

'There was a struggle and the other one struck me from behind. I remember nothing more. And when I came to I was in here and my watch was smashed,' he bit out.

'At least you weren't.' She dug up the courage to look up from her plate, her face flushed and troubled. 'Thanks for not standing by,' she muttered tightly.

'Don't thank me. What I did was foolish. He would not have fired that gun. His companion was in the way, probably already in the act of injecting you with the drug that knocked you out. Sometimes instinct betrays one badly,' he completed grimly.

He was denying the fact that he had saved her life. He didn't want her gratitude. But Bella was deeply impressed by his heroic lack of concern for his own safety. 'Instinct', he'd called it, depriving the act of anything personal. However, that did not change the fact that many men would have put themselves first sooner than risk their own life at the expense of someone who was little more than a stranger.

A stranger. Rico da Silva ought still to feel like a stranger to her, only he didn't any more. Shorn of the obvious trappings of his wealth, the male across the table was as human as she was. But she reminded herself how deceptive the situation in which they were now trapped was. They were stuck with each other. This uneasy intimacy between two people from radically different worlds had been enforced, not sought.

'If I hadn't been there, what would you have done?' she found herself asking.

'There is no profit in such conjecture.'

'You're a typical money man, aren't you?' Bella condemned helplessly. 'No such thing as answering a straight question!'

His strong features darkened. '*Estupendo* ... then I'll give it to you straight. As you screamed I was about to activate the alarm on my watch. It would have alerted my bodyguards.'

'The alarm—it would have been that loud?'

Impatience tightened his mouth, hardened his narrowed gaze. 'It is a highly sophisticated device. The kidnappers would have heard nothing, but the signal emitted would have automatically activated an emergency alert on the radios my bodyguards carry.'

'And brought them running,' she filled in, dry mouthed. 'Some watch.'

'It would also have acted as a homing device once it was activated.'

'The marvels of technology,' Bella mumbled, regarding her lettuce with a fast disappearing appetite, unable to bring herself to meet his accusing gaze. It was her fault that his watch had been smashed, her fault that he hadn't got to activate the damned thing. 'You were wired like a bomb.'

'That went off like a damp squib.'

She fumbled to think of something to say in her own defence. 'There might have been a shoot-out if your guards had come rushing back.'

'They are too highly trained for such idiocy,' Rico retorted crushingly. 'In all likelihood they would have simply tracked me and followed without revealing their presence and risking my safety.'

Bella pushed away her plate. He was telling her that she had wrecked his chances of escape. But for her persistence he would have continued to exercise restraint on that point. Rico da Silva was not the type to cry over spilt milk but, challenged beyond his tolerance threshold, he had given her what she'd asked for. And honesty had never been less welcome.

'Sorry really wouldn't cover it, would it?' she breathed jerkily.

'*No importa . . .* Who can tell what would have happened? A hundred things could have gone wrong,' he dismissed wryly. 'I bear my own share of responsibility for our plight. I dismissed my bodyguards. And had I not taken you down there you would not be here now. They were waiting for me. I have business lunches almost every day. As a potential target you are told to vary your schedule but lunch . . . lunch is difficult to vary—'

'I guess.' Bella was surprised by his sudden denial of her culpability.

Lustrous dark eyes glimmered in the dim light over her anxious face. '*Por Dios . . .* It is inexcusable that I should take my anger and frustration out on you. I owe you my apologies. I am not accustomed to this feeling of being powerless. I have always been aware that I could be the target for such a crime but I did not seriously

believe that this could happen to me. Arrogance brings
its own reward.'

'I don't see what you could have done to prevent it.'
It was hard to drag her fascinated gaze from him. He
was being so honest, so open. She had not expected that
candour from a male as sophisticated and powerful as
Rico da Silva. And the apology shook her rigid.

In her own way she saw that she had been as prejudiced
as he was. She had not been prepared for the strength
of will and purpose that he had revealed from the outset
of their imprisonment. Survival was the only item on
their agenda, he had said. He meant it; he would act on
it. But what was really driving him crazy right now, she
sensed, was the apparently foolproof setting in which
their kidnappers had chosen to place them.

'Where do you think we are?'

'If they spent the time I was unconscious driving, we
could be hundreds of miles from London. Then again,
we could still be inside the city limits.' He shifted an
expressive brown hand, his mouth tightening.

'But it's so quiet—'

'This container is set inside some sort of building. We
are not outdoors. There is some kind of roof far above
us. I was able to judge that through the airholes,' Rico
supplied, acknowledging her surprise at his knowledge.
'There is very little light in the building. It could be a
warehouse on an old industrial estate, miles from resi-
dential areas. On the other hand, it could equally well
be a barn out in the depths of the country—'

'You've really thought about this.'

'I've had more time than you and more practice. International banking is cut-throat. Thinking on my feet
comes naturally.'

Bella bent her vibrant head, amused by his assumption of mental superiority. He thought that she was
thick just because her spelling was no great shakes. No
doubt her second-hand clothing and her habit of chat-

tering when she was nervous added to his prejudice. If
he saw her paintings he might change his mind. Then
again, he might not.

Hector didn't think she was ready for a first exhibition as yet. It had been Hector who had told her that
she needed more time and more experience to develop
as an artist before she even considered trying to show
or sell her work. And Hector ought to have known what
he was talking about. In the days before he had become
a virtual recluse Hector Barsay had been a renowned
international art critic, whose opinion had been sufficient to make or break many an artistic career.

'If we're inside a barn that probably means there's a
house close by!' Her sudden animation dimmed as
quickly as it had arisen as she took that thought a step
further and felt more threatened than ever by it. 'And
if there is a house our jailers are probably inside it...'
she whispered sickly.

'*Sí.*' He did not deny the possibility. 'But the environment they have chosen for us would suggest to me
that they are equally likely to be miles away or even out
of the country by now—'

'Out of the country... leaving us *here* trapped?' Bella
had gone white.

'This was very carefully planned... all this,' Rico
stressed again, indicating their surroundings. 'They did
not employ gratuitous violence upon us—'

'I thought they were very violent.'

'They used drugs rather than brute force to subdue
us. They might have stuck us in a basement somewhere
and simply left us without food or any comfort,' he
pointed out.

'Do you think they're terrorists?'

'I think not but I could be wrong. The nervous one
did not strike me as a man used to having a gun in his
hand. The other one was more professional, more confident... He was even enjoying himself.'

Bella's sensitive stomach churned. Unlike Rico she did not have the emotional distance to assess their captor's personalities.

'To take me in that car park was a challenge, and he was a man accustomed to danger. He enjoyed the risk. Possibly a former soldier or mercenary. He had fast reactions.'

'I'm scared,' she muttered in a small voice.

Disconcertingly he reached for her clenched hand where it rested on the table. His large hand briefly engulfed hers with very welcome warmth. 'Clearly *not* a halfwit,' he said with a self-mocking edge.

'The police will be scouring the countryside for us.' Endeavouring to cheer herself up, Bella thought for the very first time of the police not as a threat but as the strong arm of the law. Investigators, protectors, *rescuers*.

There was an odd little silence. She glanced across at Rico.

'*Sì*...' He was staring down into his glass of water.

'Leaving no stone unturned—a nationwide alert,' she continued, bolstering her nerves with conviction. 'It'll be on television and radio. Everyone will know about us and someone somewhere is sure to have seen something... Maybe a few someones.'

Tight-mouthed, Rico murmured, 'Tell me about Hector.'

Thrown by the abrupt change of subject, Bella echoed, 'Hector?'

'By now he will be aware of your disappearance.'

She thought about that and shook her head. 'Not yet. We don't keep tabs like that on each other.'

'You mean he is accustomed to you not always coming home at night?' Rico phrased abrasively.

'Everyone stays over with friends sometimes. And Hector's a very private person who believes in minding his own business. He has his own very set routines and I'm not a routine sort of person,' Bella admitted. 'We don't share mealtimes very often. When he asked me to move in—'

'And when was that?'

'A year ago.'

'Where did you meet him?'

'I've known Hector for ever.' Bella grinned. 'Well, since I was fourteen.'

'*Fourteen*?' Rico grated, his dark features rigid with a response that she couldn't quite read. It looked remarkably like distaste...but why should he react that way to such a harmless piece of information?

'Why not?' Bella frowned.

'If you see no reason why not, it is not for me to comment,' Rico returned thinly. 'Where were your parents?'

'I was living with my grandfather at the time.'

'And he did not protect you from this dirty old man?' he demanded with seething distaste.

Bella's mouth fell wide in astonishment. She sprang upright. 'Are you calling Hector a dirty old man?'

'This appears to come as a big revelation to you...but *si*...yes. Such a relationship is an obscenity!'

Her green eyes fired, her temper exploding. 'You actually believe that Hector and I have a sexual relationship,' she realised in disgust. 'My God, you are stuffed full of prejudices about me! I'm sorry to disappoint your gutter assumptions, Mr da Silva, but Hector's nothing more than my landlord and a family friend—'

'A *family* friend?' Unperturbed by her anger, Rico surveyed her and merely continued to probe.

'Hector knew my father back in the sixties,' she volunteered with pronounced reluctance.

'When will he notice your absence?'

Bella drank down her glass of water, still trembling with bitter anger. 'I don't know. Not tonight anyway. He always goes to bed early and I'm often out all day.

I don't always see him at breakfast. I also work shifts, and sometimes I do extra hours if I'm asked. By the way, I'm a waitress...I'm not out trawling the streets for men to sell my body to!' she hissed at him. 'What gives with you anyway? The fact that I'm out late at night and driving a beat-up car doesn't mean I'm a tart!'

Hooded dark eyes rested on her vibrant and passionately expressive face. His mouth quirked. 'You are quite correct. But you have a quite stunning quality of raw sexuality which tends to blunt the male perceptive powers. Your looks, your walk and the husky pitch of your voice,' he murmured softly, 'add to the confusion you create.'

Wide-eyed and bewildered, Bella stared back at him. He had delivered the assessment with the same distant coolness that an employer might use when he was discussing a potential employee with personnel management. But nobody had ever talked to Bella like that before—certainly not a man. A tide of pink illuminated her porcelain-fine skin.

'And I don't think you're half as aware of the havoc you wreak as I assumed you were, *querida*.' He thrust his empty plate away and rose. 'Now I think it's time I started trying to attract attention to us again.'

He left her standing there, uncertain, confused, anger and defensiveness still contributing to her feverish tension. The first crash of metal on metal made her flinch. He was hammering the container doors with what looked like a poker. The noise hit her in shock waves. But if someone heard them, came to investigate...? What were the chances? she wondered dully. If the kidnappers had really left them alone here, that signified a fair degree of confidence that their presence was unlikely to be discovered.

Clearing up the dishes, she discovered that a bone-deep exhaustion had settled on her without her even noticing. Rico was still banging the doors, vibrations running through the whole container like thunderclaps, hurting her ears, her teeth, her head. She withstood it, bracing herself. And then he stopped, releasing his pent-up breath in a hiss.

'I'll take a turn,' Bella proffered.

He swung round, his bronzed, startlingly handsome features and curling black hair damp with perspiration. 'No need. This is allowing me to work out my anger. And you look as though you're on the brink of collapse. Why don't you lie down for a while?'

'I can do my bit just like you can,' she insisted, hovering.

'You can do it tomorrow, or in the middle of the night. The noise will carry further then. If you fall asleep I'll wake you up,' he assured her.

She gave a rueful laugh. 'Sleep with that racket?'

'Try. We need to conserve our strength to stay alert.' From the shadows he studied her with slumbrous golden eyes and, astonishingly, for the first time since it had happened, she remembered that savage embrace in the lift—the hard, hot hunger of his mouth on hers, the shatteringly sexual feel of that lean, muscular form of his crushing her to him.

'Yes,' she muttered, turning away, barely knowing what she was saying, suddenly engulfed by a level of physical awareness that she had never felt before, struggling to thrust that intimate memory away again.

'You remind me of a marmalade cat,' he said abruptly. 'It's the hair.'

'I can see you slinking through the undergrowth, stalking your prey.'

'I haven't heard that one before.' She forced a laugh and vanished back through the curtain. At the sink she washed her face and hands, dried herself on one of the two rough, faded towels available, peered at the still wrapped toothbrush and paste. The kidnappers hadn't planned to make Rico too uncomfortable. The conviction was soothing.

'Can we share a toothbrush?' she called in a lull in the noise.

'If we can share a bed we can share a toothbrush,' Rico murmured lazily.

But they were not going to share that bed. They would take turns. Very democratic. Very sensible. One asleep, one awake and alert. And always that background of deafening noise. Thud, thud, crash, crash. It was impossible that anyone could fall asleep against that background. Having removed her boots and her tights in the kitchen section, Bella walked back to the bed. Covertly undoing a couple of the buttons on her fitted jacket, she slid below the blanket, rested her head on the pillow, and turned away from him towards the wall.

But still his image lingered behind her lowered eyelids, stamped there like a cattle brand seared into her flesh. Involuntarily she remembered the kiss, relived the wildness he had unleashed—from inside her, from inside him. Trying to fly off the top of a tall building would have been less dangerous, less foolhardy. She shivered. The fire had simply taken over, burning out all self-control.

No man had ever made her feel like that. And she didn't ever want to feel like that again. Passion was greedy and mindless. Passion was lust, a purely physical thing which had no staying power. Bella knew that some people were lucky enough to find both love *and* passion in a lasting relationship but those people were in the minority. Many more mistook infatuation for love and then wondered why their feelings faded so quickly. But Bella knew the difference and knew what to guard against.

Both of her parents had been passionate people and neither Cleo nor Ivan had controlled that side of their nature. Neither of them had ever managed to sustain a

stable relationship, not with each other and not with
anybody else. Their love affairs had been volatile, short-
lived and unfulfilling. Why? Because they had been
greedy, impatient and always afraid that the grass might
be greener with someone else.

Bella was determined not to fall into the same trap.
Yes, she had needs and drives just like any other young,
healthy woman, but she wanted to choose her life partner
with her intellect, not with her body. It dawned on her
that she had not thought of Griff in almost twenty-four
hours. She was shaken. But then, it had been a frantic
and worrying twenty-four hours, and Griff had hurt her,
and no doubt she was already in the recovery phase.
Bella's feelings shut down fast when she was disappointed or betrayed.

But she had been very fond of Griff. She had enjoyed
his company, respected his intelligence and believed that
his outlook and expectations of life matched her own.
That, she had foolishly assumed, had been a sufficient
basis on which to build a good relationship. Only it
hadn't been enough for Griff. She had refused to go to
bed with him in the absence of any deeper commitment
on his part.

That giggle in the background on the phone had told
her that he had been finding physical entertainment else-
where. Griff had made his choice but she knew him well
enough to know that he would still believe that he could
string her along. But Bella wouldn't allow that. It was
over. Griff was immature, clearly not yet ready to think
in terms of permanence in spite of all the things he had
said to the contrary.

That sorted out tidily in her mind, Bella contrived to
do what she had not believed possible. She fell asleep.
And she awakened to a situation that was entirely new
to her.

She was lying on top of a living, breathing pillow. Her
nostrils flared at the clean, soapy scent of warm male.

Her breasts were crushed against a rough-haired chest,
her cheek pillowed in the hollow of a smooth shoulder,
and her pelvis was in direct contact with the thrust of a
very masculine arousal. In the darkness her head flew
up, her eyes wide with consternation.

Her breasts were crushed against a rough, natural-dark-
ness cushioned in the hollow of a smooth shoulder
and her hips was in snug contact with the thrust of a
very masculine anatomy. In the instant her head flew
up, her eyes wide

CHAPTER FOUR

A HAND pressed her back down again. 'Go back to sleep,'
Rico breathed tautly.

'Like hell I will!' Bella gasped in alarm, trying to rise
but thwarted by the powerful arm wrapped around her
hips.

'*Dios*! Relax,' he hissed with raw impatience.

'You've just got to be kidding! You're in bed with
me!'

'*Madre de Dios*, it's four in the morning—'

'Time I got up and took my turn at thumping walls!'

Both arms closed round her. 'Forget it,' he groaned.
'It's the middle of the night. I need sleep. If you start,
I won't get any.'

'I am not sharing this bed with you!'

'What do you think I am—a rapist?' he growled
incredulously.

'How...do...I...know?' she fielded with growing
fury. 'You're not wearing any clothes!'

'As I have only one set I refuse to go to bed in them.
But I am *not* naked.' Closing his hand round one of
hers, he thrust it down to the hard jut of his hips,
splaying her fingers against the band of cloth there to
prove his point.

Bella nearly went into orbit at the intimacy of the
gesture. 'How dare you?' she screeched, snatching her
hand back even though she hadn't been anywhere near
the danger zone that she was already outrageously aware
of.

He expelled his breath in a resonant hiss of exasperation. 'You are not that naïve. I am a man, lying in bed

with a half-naked woman on top of me. I'm not a corpse, devoid of all sexual response. But I have no intention of making love to you.'

'I don't believe you!' she bit out, rigid as a stick of rock, holding her entire length taut in a fruitless endeavour to lessen the points of contact between them.

'I am fully in control of my sexual urges,' he extended grittily into her ear. 'But not my temper, I warn you.'

'I don't trust you,' she whispered back with venomous bite, infuriated by the position in which she found herself. 'I could fall asleep and you—'

'Oh, I do believe you would wake up if I touched you. I believe that I can safely say a woman has never slept through my attentions!'

'Don't be disgusting! Let me go!'

He gave vent to something rough and charged in Spanish and moved with an abruptness that took her completely by surprise. Suddenly she was flipped onto her back and Rico was lying above her instead, their positions reversed without warning. Before she could open her startled lips to demand an explanation he took her mouth in a surge of angry passion.

And what happened next she definitely wasn't prepared to deal with. As his tongue drove into the moist interior she had already accidentally opened to him she was seized by an explosive wave of excitement. It left her dizzy and stripped of every coherent thought. The intensity of her own response electrified her, opening up another world that was full of unbearable physical temptation. She returned the kiss with a kind of wondering innocence, arching her head back to deepen the pressure, involuntarily greedy and inviting more.

'*Por Dios...*' he groaned raggedly, his lean, hard body coming down into abrupt and abrasive contact with her yielding curves where, seconds earlier, he had held himself at a distance. 'I—'

Driven entirely by instinct, Bella speared her unsteady
fingers into the thick silk of his hair and held him down
to her, tracing the shape of his head in an exploratory
caress. Touching had never felt so good, never felt so
necessary. Entrapped by the discovery and fired by the
leaping, unfamiliar energy sizzling along her nerve-
endings, she threw herself with natural generosity into
the conflagration of their mouths' second meeting a split-
second later.

Incredible heat rose from deep inside her, making her
body shake and quiver with the sheer power of what she
was feeling. He pulled her to him as he slid onto his side,
his hand curving to the pouting thrust of one full breast,
inadequately protected by the thin lace cup of her bra.
And then the barrier was inexplicably no longer there,
his fingers shaping her naked, sensitised flesh with an
expertise that made her gasp. In the darkness she felt
him move, and the yearning peak of one engorged nipple
was brushed by the tip of his tongue and then engulfed
by his mouth.

Bella moaned, and jerked as though she had been
electrified. All she could hear was the rasp of her tortured breathing, the thunder of her heartbeat. Sensation
so intense that it came close to torment had her in its
grip. She was out of control, sensed it, felt it, *knew* it,
and being out of control was something Bella never, ever
allowed herself to be with a man. The shock of that realisation awakened her brain from its slumber, and in
panic she wrenched herself free by rolling backwards.

'*No!*' she slung at him from between clenched teeth
as she hit the hard floor with a force that hurt. Rolling
over, feeling the nakedness of her back and breasts in
dismayed confusion, she fumbled out blindly to feel the
wall opposite the bed and sat there, hugging her knees
and shivering as the light went on.

'*Madre de Dios . . .*' Rico hissed, studying her with incandescent golden eyes from the vantage point of the bed. 'What the hell are you playing at?'

'Please return my clothing to me.' She lowered her eyes and studied her raised knees, embarrassment and an unfamiliar self-loathing assailing her. But still she could see that strong-boned, hard face, brought alive by those astonishingly passionate eyes of his, the lithe, powerful symmetry of his bronzed, beautifully masculine body. Her nails dug into her skin in angry, fearful confusion as she fought to wipe out that unbelievably intense and detailed image.

Her jacket and her bra landed in a heap beside her bare toes. She skidded upright, twisting away from him, and dug her arms shakily into the sleeves of the jacket, ignoring the bra because *he* was watching her. She hadn't even noticed that he had removed both articles while she had been in his arms. It was a small point but somehow it underlined just how far her control and awareness had slipped and emphasised how complete had been his.

Smooth bastard, she reflected shakily, deciding that you couldn't know where you were with a guy possessed of that variety of sexual expertise. At least with the ones who grabbed and clutched you got fair warning of their intentions.

'You are behaving as though I attacked you,' he grated in a furious undertone.

'You started it, I finished it. Let's leave it there,' she muttered unsteadily, with her back still cravenly turned to him.

'I did not do *anything*—'

'That I didn't encourage you to do,' Bella completed in a grudging interruption. 'I know.'

There was a smouldering silence.

'If you acknowledge that—' and his accented drawl told her just how astonished he was that she had made that acknowledgement '—then why—?'

'My hormones are out of sync... or something.'

'*Qué dices*...?' Now he sounded slightly dazed.

Bella forced herself to turn around. It took courage. 'It's this situation... the proximity, the misleading intimacy, the tension we are both under,' she offered. 'I'm sorry I let it go so far but neither one of us can want to wake up in the morning trapped with a sleazy one-night stand we can't escape from—'

'"Sleazy"?' he echoed in disbelief.

'Listen, I am the girl whom just a few hours ago you believed to be shacked up with an old guy of seventy.' Having given the gentle reminder, Bella tilted her chin. 'And sex without emotional involvement or commitment is sleazy in my book. I don't know you well enough to say whether or not it would be in yours. But, if you're like most of the men I meet, you don't intellectualise much over taking sex where it's offered. You just *do* it and you don't have the sensitivity to feel bad about it.'

She gave a dismissive little shrug, the absorbing focus of his stunned scrutiny. 'But that's OK. I don't judge men on that. That's just the way nature programmed you to behave. Survival of the species and all that.'

His brilliant dark eyes shimmered, his facial muscles stiff with sudden hauteur, a faint but perceptible flush overlying his hard cheekbones. 'I did not emerge from the primordial soup within recent memory,' he gritted from between even white teeth.

'Only you don't think on your feet when you're in bed with a half-naked woman and feeling randy—'

'I refuse to believe I am hearing this!'

Bella lifted his jacket, which he had laid across the chair, and began to empty the pockets.

'What are you doing?' he murmured in a seriously taut tone, his accent thick.

'I'm going to use your jacket as a blanket for an hour and then maybe, when you've managed to drop off, I can take up the door-bashing again.'

'Don't be ridiculous. Come back to bed. I will not lay a finger on you,' he swore icily.

'It's not a very good idea for us to share that bed right now, Rico. Take it from me,' Bella muttered feelingly, 'it would just be asking for trouble.'

'If you are determined to treat me like some sort of lech—'

She cleared her throat awkwardly and mumbled, 'No, that's not what I'm trying to say. I'm simply trying to be sensible—'

'*Trust me!*' he bit out, with audible difficulty, anger and a whole host of other emotions she didn't recognise fracturing his diction.

'I'd like to... I'd really like to, but I don't trust me either,' she admitted in a stifled confession which she felt that, in all fairness, she owed him.

'You don't trust...? Ah.' A faint purr of complacency softened his drawl. 'I thought you didn't go for dark men?'

'There's an exception to every rule... but maybe Dracula could start looking appealing in this set-up.'

He sighed. 'I have never been so tired in my life. Come back to bed. I promise you... you will be safe as a nun handcuffed to a priest in captivity.'

Bella sent him a dubious glance. He had slumped back down again, black lashes fanned down on his cheekbones. Exhaustion emanated from every line of his long, muscular body. 'Go to sleep, Rico,' she whispered, a strange little arrow of tenderness piercing her. 'Just go to sleep.'

'I can't leave you on the floor...' he mumbled thickly.

'I've slept on a lot of floors in my time.' She sighed, thinking that no two individuals could have been more different.

She sat on the chair, wrapped in his jacket, watching him sleep. The exception to the rule, she reflected tautly. Well, you've been well and truly rocked off your smug perch this time, Bella.

She was locked in a container with the only male who had ever managed to penetrate her physical and mental defences. That scared her; that really did scare her.

Men flocked to Bella like bees round a honey pot but nine out of ten invariably wanted what she didn't want to give. Being a sex object was no compliment. Either she dated for fun and friendship or she quite cheerfully chose and dated a man who impressed her as having the kind of qualities she would like to find in a husband. There was nothing in between for Bella—no infatuations, no affairs, no regrets. She was determined not to give her heart unless she felt safe and secure.

And until now passion had left her alone and untouched by any inconvenient cravings. Saying no when lovemaking went beyond a certain boundary had never been a problem for her, and she had always sensibly ensured that she did not give any man the ammunition to accuse her of being a tease. Bella believed in being honest and fair with the opposite sex. It had not crossed her mind that some day a man might touch her and with every fibre of her being she might crave the passion he inspired inside her, and crave it with such intensity that she almost broke the rules she had lived by for so long.

Rico da Silva had taught her differently. He had shattered her control as easily as a child smashed an egg and with a similar lack of care or regard for the consequences. And did she blame him for that? Neither of them might emerge from this container alive, she thought, with a shiver of fear. When two people were attracted to each other and forced into such intimacy the act of sex might seem a very small thing to share in comparison to that hard reality...

But Bella was too conscious of her own vulnerability—this strange, new and scary vulnerability that she was feeling. Rico da Silva disturbed her more than any other male she had ever met. He was clever; he was strong; he was unexpectedly candid about his own emotions. And he also attracted her more violently than she had ever believed possible.

In the dim light she looked at him lying in the bed, and knew that lying in that bed with him would result in a conflagration of passion which she would find very difficult to handle. Yet she also knew that on some dark, deep level inside herself, unexplored until this moment, she wanted that passion very, very badly.

Why? Their situation, as she had told him? No, it was something more than that. He was so different from her. In every way. And that fact in itself fascinated her. Nowhere did they share anything in common—background, nationality, status, education, income, outlook.

Rico would have been quite capable of making love to her and forgetting her existence one second after he'd achieved the satisfaction of physical release. Rico was ruthless, single-minded, a sexual predator in this particular tight corner. Rico wouldn't have felt awkward over the breakfast-table. On his scale it would have been a minor event, unimportant when set against survival.

But Bella was not half as tough on the inside as she liked to pretend on the outside. Her outer shell of careless insouciance had been formed in the hard school of her childhood—with the slow, painful acceptance that her father didn't give a damn about her, and that her mother dragged her about in her wake not out of choice but out of necessity, because there was nobody else to take responsibility. And when one day the possession of that child, now grown to an awkward thirteen-year-old threatened to come between Cleo and her latest man Cleo had dumped her on her grandfather, who hadn't even known of her existence.

Bella had learnt not to let people get too close. She had learnt to protect her inner self from invasion. On the surface she was open, but inside herself she knew she told nobody anything which mattered. And now she could feel that reserve being threatened, her essential emotional distance coming under attack. Griff hadn't hurt her, Griff had disappointed her, but she had the horrible suspicion that Rico da Silva had the power to tear her inside out...

'*Por Dios*, what the hell are you doing?'

Bella jumped and unsealed her lips from the cold metal, her shoulders and arms aching from the awkward stance she had repeatedly taken up over the past few hours. She teetered on the chair, her legs stiff, and she would have fallen if a pair of strong arms hadn't closed round her and lowered her down to the floor.

Rico was staring without comprehension at the line of tins, deprived of their labels, on the table. An incredulous frown was dug between his ebony brows as he abruptly noticed his open wallet, now emptied of the considerable amount of paper money that he had been carrying. One lean hand reached out and snatched at the single rolled banknote still lying there. He opened it up and read the message carefully printed on it.

' "Help. We're in the container",' he said out loud.

'I took the labels off the tins and tore them up and wrote on them first,' she explained. 'Then I pushed them through the biggest airhole. Then I had to blow to make them move. I'm hoping that some of them made it down onto the ground, or that there's enough of a draught out there to take them off the roof. If anyone comes in they might notice them. That was when I thought of seeing what you had in your wallet—'

'*Had* being the operative word.' Rico studied her with intent, narrowed dark eyes.

'Sorry...but a rolled-up twenty-pound note is far more likely to be noticed than a torn piece of label off a tin,' she pointed out.

'*Sì*...' Still staring at her, he pushed long fingers somewhat unsteadily through his luxuriant hair and handed her the final note. Bella got back on the chair and posted it up into the world outside their prison. 'I should have thought of this...' he murmured tautly, gravely.

'You think you have the monopoly on ideas around here?' She laughed wryly. 'It's a far-out hope that someone will innocently walk in here, pick up one of those notes and release us—'

'But not impossible. It's a clever idea.'

'Not if the ground out there is already littered or covered with debris, but who knows?' Oddly embarrassed by his level of scrutiny, she turned away. 'What do you want for breakfast?'

'I think I owe you breakfast. You let me sleep for hours.' He caught her wrist to examine her watch and groaned in disbelief. 'It's after twelve...almost lunchtime! Why didn't you wake me?'

'Relax. I did a lot of poker-bashing on and off.' Bella flexed aching muscles, but she was horrendously conscious of those cool fingers still anchored to the tender inner skin of her wrist. 'You slept through it. You needed the rest. I think whatever drug they used on us was still pretty much in both our systems until we could sleep it off. Where did you find that poker anyway?'

'Stuffed behind the stove—an oversight on their part.' His oddly abbreviated speech was matched by the blatant intensity of his continuing appraisal. His lashes dipped, showing only a glimmer of a pure, glinting gold, and he breathed in almost jerkily.

Her mouth ran dry, her heartbeat accelerating in a sudden, alarming surge. The atmosphere was thick with explosive tension. It had come out of nowhere and inexplicably, although her brain screamed at her to move away, her feet were welded to the floor in front of him. She couldn't take her eyes off him. A pulse-beat of awareness vibrated between them. It was so powerful that it drained her of self-will.

'I've been thinking,' she said in a rather high-pitched voice, fighting for concentration, desperate to break the silence. 'It's more likely that we're in a warehouse than a barn. This container wasn't plumbed in with water just for us. Those fitments in there have been *in situ* for years. This place has been used maybe as an office... or some sort of permanent site hut, I reckon... What do you think?' By the time she reached the end of that question she was spitting out words so fast that they ran into each other.

He wasn't listening. He muttered something rough and yet soft in Spanish, and just as suddenly reached for her. As possessed by that terrifying strong need to physically connect as he was, Bella made no demur. Lost in the slumbrous demand of his golden gaze, she was mindless. He took her mouth with a hunger that burned like flames of fire over her unprotected skin.

And yet she craved that fire, needed that fire as she needed oxygen to live. Her hands gripped his broad shoulders, loving the heat of his flesh through the fine shirt. She pushed against him as he crushed her to him, her breasts flattened to the hard wall of his chest, already heavy with a sensitivity and an anticipation which he alone had taught her to feel. Her body remembered him with every newly awakened sense.

His mouth on hers was a source of unbearable pleasure. She was inflamed by it, driven with incredible speed to a pitch of desire strong enough to make her legs tremble and offer only the most fragile support. Every stab of his tongue intensified the drowning excitement that was fast claiming her. She kissed him back with an intensity of response that utterly controlled her,

her hands sliding under his unbuttoned shirt, smoothing wonderingly over the flexing muscles of the satin-smooth skin of his back.

He dragged his lips from hers with a fevered imprecation and looked down at her, his breathing roughly audible. Hot golden eyes raked her flushed, vibrant face, and he set her free with an abruptness that felt like an amputation. Bella was less able to pull back from the extraordinary power he could exert over her. Every time it happened it was a revelation, and, instead of it strengthening her resistance, she found herself further weakened by the repetition.

Rico lounged back against the edge of the table, tension screaming from every poised angle of him. He appraised her with fiercely narrowed eyes, his sensual mouth compressed in a hard line. He looked like a pirate, his jaw-line obscured by a blue shadow of dark stubble. Her own skin was tingling from that abrasive contact. She raised a shaky hand to her reddened lips, feeling as though she had been branded, feeling as though she would never, ever be the same again.

'I can keep my hands off you,' he asserted with almost ferocious bite.

No, you can't and the knowledge is killing you. Bella read in his clear eyes the frustration, the anger he couldn't hide. This was a male accustomed to calling every shot, staying in control, never leaping before he looked. She remembered the tidiness of his desk and the incredulity with which he had emerged from the cluttered chaos of the interior of the Skoda that first night. Rico was one of those very organised and disciplined individuals who very rarely made an uncalculated move...and she threw him off balance and he didn't like that one bit more than she did.

'This will not happen again,' he drawled flatly.

'I know... you don't want to seem like a snob but I'm really *not* your type,' she remarked brittlely. 'And you're not my type either. Let's leave it at that.'

His teeth clenched. 'I am not a snob!'

'You just like to think that everyone's your equal from the safe cocoon of your bloody great limousine? Now you know that you don't think that, Rico. You're rich and you're successful and you probably come from a rich, priveleged family. You have power and financial clout. You probably get a lot of respect and an equal amount of grovelling flattery and servility. You're bound to have a good opinion of yourself. And you definitely don't expect to be attracted to an Essex girl who writes illiterate prose!'

'*Basta... enough!*' he slashed back at her rawly. 'How can you talk like this?'

'And that bothers you even more, doesn't it? People don't say stuff like that right out where you come from.' Bella treated him to a grim little smile, her beautiful face cynically set, masking the pain she was feeling. 'But what the hell...? I'm not about to change myself for your benefit!'

'You don't know what you're talking about.' He sent her a glittering glance that was alight with impatience and anger. 'I drew back because I had no other choice. I cannot protect you. Even if you are on the Pill you have no supply with you. I could get you pregnant, and that is a risk that neither of us can want!'

The blood drained from her face, leaving her pale, and then abruptly her skin flamed again with a stupid embarrassment she couldn't help. Hurriedly she turned away from him, shaken that he could reason so coolly about an unlikely possibility, the mere mention of which infuriated her. Did no woman ever say no to Rico da Silva? Did he think he was irresistible? Did he really imagine that she would have been foolish enough to let matters proceed to the point where the risk of pregnancy could have become a consideration?

'It wasn't going to go that far, believe me!'

'I wish I had your confidence—'

'All I did was let you kiss me, for heaven's sake! That doesn't mean I was about to jump into bed with you!' she hissed, slamming into the fridge, unwilling to look at him because she was so outraged by his assumption that she was easily available should he choose to exert sufficient persuasion.

'Keep quiet. Talking about it doesn't help,' he breathed in a sudden, savage undertone that brutally ruptured the heavy silence, sentencing her to nervous paralysis. 'I ache to have you... *Santa María*, I am in torment. I want to rip your clothes off and fall on you like an animal, and in all my adult life I have never been so challenged to retain control and consider consequences!'

Bella straightened and slowly turned. Rico glowered back at her, the raw reality of what he was telling her etched in the ferocious set of his dark, startlingly handsome features.

'And if you did not want me the problem would not be there. I would never touch a woman without her consent,' he continued forcefully. 'But every time you look at me I see the same hunger in you.'

'I—'

'Do not deny it,' he cut in grimly. 'And that we should be distracted by such primitive instincts when our very lives are at risk outrages my intelligence!'

'It's the fact that we're trapped here,' she muttered, shattered by his candour, devastated by the manner in which he was still looking at her, and shamefully lost in a colourful image of him ripping her clothes off and her liking it. Dear God, what was happening to her? What was happening to them both?

'*No digas disparates!*'

'In English?'

'Don't talk rubbish.' He flashed her an exasperated glance, his beautifully shaped mouth twisting. 'I felt exactly the same way in my office. Why do you think I was so determined to take you to the police?'

'I had to be punished for attracting you? Are you a sadist or something?'

'Since I met you I have been *crazy*!' he raked back at her in a sudden explosion of raw, passionate resentment. 'I don't know myself any more!'

Swinging on his heel, he strode through the beaded curtain. A second later she heard the fiery assault of the poker on the container doors and couldn't help smiling to herself. Rico was as disconcerted by the attraction between them as she was. That made her feel less threatened and more in control. Neither of them wanted anything to happen. Between them they ought to be capable of behaving like civilised adults and observing proper boundaries in spite of this horribly intimate and suffocating prison.

But, dear heaven, when he threw off the ice-cool front and let the tiger roar, she thought distractedly, Rico was quite shockingly volatile—yet another trait she ran a mile from in men. Only then did it cross her mind that she found the same trait astonishingly, paradoxically attractive when Rico revealed it. The sheer elemental physicality and passion which he suppressed and controlled with cold intellect fascinated her.

She made sandwiches for lunch—no sense in letting the bread go stale. Rico sank down on the other side of the table, his every graceful movement catching her attention. She averted her eyes to her glass of milk. 'Do you have a family out there worrying about you?' she asked abruptly.

'My parents are dead. I have an older sister, who's married with a family, but she lives in Spain.'

'I imagine the police will have carried the news that far by now.' Bella sighed.

Rico seemed to hesitate. '*Sí...*'

He reverted to his own language only when tense. No doubt he was disturbed by the idea of his sister's current state of terror on his behalf.

'Are you close?'

'Yes.'

Bella was determined to keep on talking. Maybe conversation would keep other, far more dangerous undertones at bay. 'You're Spanish, aren't you?'

'My father was Portuguese but my mother was Spanish. I grew up in Andalusia.'

'Rich?'

'Rich,' he conceded almost apologetically.

Involuntarily she glanced up and collided with a positively dazzling half-smile that gave her a seductive glimpse of another Rico entirely—a Rico with a sense of humour and considerable charm. That smile made her feel curiously light-headed. 'What were your parents like? Distant?'

'Not at all.' He looked surprised by the suggestion. 'We were a happy family but I was born late in their lives. My father died when I was a teenager, my mother a couple of years ago—'

'So what age are you?'

'Thirty-two...far too old for you,' he murmured in unwelcome addition.

'Look, we're not going to talk about things like that!' Bella snapped, emerald-green eyes flashing reproach and reproof. 'You're an...Aquarius...right?'

Rico frowned. 'Ah...astrology. *Sí*.'

'We should avoid each other like the plague,' she told him morosely. 'It's a combustible combination.'

'I do not require a horoscope to know that, *gatita*,' he returned with dark satire. 'So tell me about your background.'

'Forget it. It would give you indigestion.'

'I would like to know. Who were your parents?'

Bella stiffened. Of course he didn't mean 'who' in the worldly sense. He certainly wouldn't be expecting to hear a name that he might recognise. She lifted her vibrant head, her sultry mouth compressing. 'My father was Ivan Sinclair.'

His winged ebony brows drew together in unconcealed surprise. 'The artist?'

'My mother was one of his models. They had an affair. I was the result.' She wondered why she had told him something that she usually kept very much to herself.

His dark visage was set in uninformative lines. 'There was no marriage?'

'Ivan didn't believe in marriage. He visited Cleo on and off for a while after I was born but that eventually ground to a halt,' she admitted. 'I didn't see him again until I was thirteen. And my mother initiated that meeting. She wanted him to take charge of me... It was a really stupid idea...'

The silence stretched and then Rico murmured, 'What happened?'

'Nothing much.' With a jerky shrug she got up and began to clear the table. 'He was furious at being put on the spot. He accused her of trying to blackmail him, even tried to say I wasn't his... He was quite pathetic actually. He was no hero.'

'He had a lot of talent.'

'But, let's face it, he was much better known as a drunk and a womaniser.' Bella stated the obvious for him.

'Scarcely a suitable guardian for a thirteen-year-old. Why did your mother even consider such an arrangement?'

She turned back to him, her beautiful face strong and her expression clear. 'She had a lover who didn't want a kid hanging around,' she said bluntly. 'But her visit to Ivan wasn't a total disappointment. He coughed up some cash to get rid of us; she bought a new van and dumped me with my grandfather instead.'

An ebony brow quirked. 'A new van?'

'My mother was a traveller. She wasn't born to the life, but then few are.' Bella sighed. 'She left home when she was eighteen. She was a hippie. Gramps said she was wild. He threw her out after an argument and then regretted it, but he didn't see her again until she showed up with me twenty-odd years later. She was only involved with Ivan for a couple of years and then she met some guy with a lorry and took to the road—'

'For how long... until you were thirteen?'

She nodded.

'But you must have settled somewhere at some stage?'

'Never for longer than a month.'

'What about your education?'

She smiled. 'I started that at thirteen.'

'It must have been an appalling life.' Rico frowned at her, his consternation palpable.

'I didn't know anything else. Sometimes it was fun.' But her expressive eyes shadowed. She was thinking of the hunger and the cold and the wet, the lack of hygiene and privacy, the raw hostility of their reception everywhere they went. Travellers were not welcome visitors in any locality.

'Time I bashed the poker,' she announced abruptly, suddenly bewildered and alarmed by the extent to which she had allowed him to draw her out. She never told people about that old life if she could help it, and could not understand why she had revealed so much to him. It was none of his business.

She strode down to the container doors and lifted the poker. She had only struck the metal a few times when another sound broke through in startling, shattering response—a series of sharp, zinging thuds. The poker fell from her nerveless fingers. She spun round, heard Rico behind her, then they were suddenly plunged into darkness and he was dragging her down on the bed. 'Keep quiet,' he urged in a raw breath of warning.

'*But—*' Had he gone crazy? Someone was out there—someone who could open those doors and set them free!

'Those were bullets.' Rico's hands framed her cheek-bones in the darkness and she fell back, sick and weak with terror.

CHAPTER FIVE

THERE was a loud thud up on the roof. Bella shivered violently as she heard the unmistakable sound of feet walking up and down above them. Nausea filled her stomach. Somebody laughed. There was a roaring in her eardrums. Her heart threatened to burst from her ribcage. For just a little while she had managed to close out the fear but now it was back with a vengeance.

Rico rolled over, pinning her body almost protectively beneath his. She could feel the splintering tension coursing through him and abruptly she closed her arms around him, needing that reassuring contact with every fibre of her being. She felt so small, so frighteningly powerless. They were caught like rats in a trap, wholly at the mercy of their captors.

Her breath rasped in her aching throat as there was another thud, then nothing. The silence dragged past on leaden feet until it seemed to thunder in her straining ears.

'He's gone,' Rico grated.

'How do you know? He could be standing out th-there just waiting for us to make more noise...and then he might come in!' she gasped strickenly.

'I doubt it. I suspect he was only checking on us...but for the moment we keep quiet.'

'Bastard,' Bella mumbled, still shaking like a leaf in a high wind, her face buried in the hollow between his shoulder and his throat. Her nostrils flared on the warm, musky scent of him, already so reassuringly familiar. 'You imagine you're coping and then...then they take that away and remind you how it really is!'

'The ransom will be paid, no questions asked—'

'But maybe the police won't allow that!'

'The police are unlikely to be actively involved at this stage.'

'*What*?' In the darkness her dazed eyes flew wide.

Rico shifted and switched on the light where it sat on the chair by the bed. 'My bank will pay up. The police will stand back at this early stage. That is standard procedure. Publicity could be our death warrant. Scared kidnappers get more dangerous...'

Bella met his shimmering gold eyes, absorbed the wry, apologetic curve of his mouth as he released her from his weight and coiled back from her. He had allowed her to believe that the police were out there searching for them because that had appeared to keep up her spirits. 'Oh, God...' she whispered shakily as reality sank in.

'*Lo siento, gatita*...I'm sorry.'

'I guess if that's the best approach...'

'At the highest level the police will certainly have been informed of the kidnapping,' Rico asserted. 'But I would imagine that at this point they are merely waiting to see how the situation develops.'

'And if what you euphemistically call "the situation" develops into tragedy, then they'll be more actively involved!' Bella could not resist saying.

His jaw-line clenched. 'Don't talk like that!'

'You want me to maintain a positive outlook when we're stuck here like sitting ducks inside a metal tomb with some maniac taking pot-shots at us for fun?' A shrill, hysterical edge had entered her voice.

'Every occurrence increases our knowledge of the environment outside,' Rico intoned, staring her down with icy night-dark eyes.

'I beg your pardon?' she said incredulously.

'We're wasting time and energy with that poker,' he imparted with grim emphasis. 'He would not have fired that gun at this hour of the day had there been the remotest chance of anyone hearing the gunshots.'

'Oh...Rico...that is *so* comforting to know!' she spat back in helpless disbelief.

'I do not think that our lives are in any immediate danger,' he grated.

'You also thought that our kidnappers might be out of the country!'

'*Por Dios* ... pull yourself together! This far you have acted with commendable courage.'

Bella could feel her control unravelling as fast and as inescapably as a cotton reel of thread thrown down a steep hill. 'Not quite what you expected from me, I gather. Well, I'd appreciate it more if you showed a little human sensitivity, instead of acting like Mr Macho all the time...even when we're in the middle of a nightmare!' Her voice rose steeply on the last words, fractured by the sob choking her throat.

'I don't think you'd appreciate it if I was sitting here paralysed with fear!'

The sobs she was frantically struggling to suppress overcame her. She bowed her head, ashamed of the weakness, and wrapped her arms round herself. Tears streamed down her cheeks. He touched her damp chin with a not quite steady forefinger and then, with a muttered, vicious imprecation, reached for her, unpeeling her arms and hauling her close.

She needed that contact. She needed that warmth... She needed *him*. Caught up in the charge of an explosive surge of feeling, she pressed her mouth feverishly to the angular curve of his stubbled jaw-line.

She felt him tense but there was an unstoppable flood of emotion suddenly churning about inside her. Her hands slid up, her fingers shyly splaying across his blunt cheekbones in a wondering caress. As she held him she looked at him with darkened green eyes full of new self-knowledge and a kind of helpless joy that was insanity,

but which she couldn't help. Her feelings were so intense
that they consumed her.

'I don't trust myself this close,' Rico breathed roughly.

'Trust your instincts,' she whispered, and she dropped
her hands, then hesitated in a momentary agony of un-
certainty before her fingers found the buttons on her
jacket and began to release them.

'Bella...'

Her pale skin burned under the golden flare of his
arrested gaze, but the driving need to give, to share, was
far more powerful than the fleeting recall of her own
sexual inexperience.

'This is just you and me,' she reasoned in a breath of
sound as the jacket slid off her shoulders, her slender
form quivering with sudden awareness of her own daring.
'And this is what I want.'

Every poised inch of his lithe, powerful length exuded
the raw force of his tension. Bella looked bravely back
at him, still clothed, but naked to the world as she had
never before allowed herself to be. It was a risk she had
to take, a leap of faith, and even though she knew that
she might regret her own unquestioning generosity she
also knew that she would regret it for the rest of her life
if she simply hid behind her own insecurities.

'Si...' He moved with an abruptness then that shattered her—reaching for her, dragging her into his arms,
every restraint overpowered by the hunger which blazed
in incandescent gold from his fierce gaze. 'No regrets?'

He wanted a passport to freedom before he even
touched her. Pain trammelled through her. She might
have turned away then, devastated by the reality of how
little he offered and too proud to take on such terms,
but he closed his mouth in devouring passion over hers
and the ability to be rational was violently torn from
her.

He invaded the moist interior of her mouth, his
probing tongue a raw, masculine imitation of an infi-

nitely more intimate penetration. She trembled, every physical sense leaping into automatic response. Control was wrested from her without remorse. He unleashed the turbulent force of his desire on her and she drowned mindlessly in the tidal wave of her own shock. It was no slow, gentle seduction which took account of her innocence.

'You're a witch, *querida* . . .' Rico groaned. 'I am no saint to resist such enticement.'

'Enticement'? Some faint shred of reasoning absorbed the word, shrank from it. But he took her mouth again, made love to it, enveloped her in the staggering surge of her own helpless excitement. He lifted his dark head and she opened her heavy eyes. He had bared her breasts. The pale mounds rose in shameless supplication to his heated appraisal.

'You are so beautiful.' He cupped her sensitive flesh with firm hands, his smouldering golden scrutiny raking over her as a flush of pink crept up over her cheekbones.

He bent his head. She watched him, shameless in the grip of her own anticipation and yet so afraid that in some sense she might not meet his expectations.

The tip of his tongue skidded down the valley between her breasts before circling the engorged thrust of one pink nipple. She gasped, her lashes sweeping down, her back arching. Thought was suspended. The erotic tug of his mouth on the sensitised buds was unbearably erotic. Her hands rose of their own volition and speared into his hair, caressing him, holding him to her as the sweet torment of her own arousal plunged her into ever deeper response. In all her life she had never dreamt that such pleasure existed.

She was so hot that she couldn't stay still. His fingers smoothed over the quivering tautness of her stomach and located the tangle of curls at the junction of her thighs. Her whole body jerked, out of control. Her breath rasped dry in her throat, her thighs parting in a

spasm of intolerable need. He laughed softly and covered
her mouth again, teasing this time, nibbling and tormenting with devastating expertise.

Instinctively she moved against him, her hips rising.
He explored the damp, silken warmth at the very heart
of her, every expert caress making her sob with the crazed
heat of that intimate pleasure. Lost in the depths of an
extraordinary passion, she was at the peak of an intense
excitement, tortured by the desperate ache of
unfulfilment.

He shifted over her then, ravishing her swollen lips
one more time, and then, abruptly, he drew her up to
him with impatient hands and plunged inside her. She
hadn't expected the pain that tore at her as he entered
her. Her shocked eyes flew wide and she bit her tongue
so hard that she tasted blood in her mouth.

'*Madre de Dios*!' Shattered golden eyes held hers, and
then his teeth clenched as the momentum of his own
desire made him drive deeper still, his swollen shaft
forging a path through the tender tissue that had sought
to deny him.

'That hurts!' Bella panted.

With a sharp intake of breath he stilled, and long
fingers knotted painfully into her tumbled hair. 'I didn't
know!'

She saw the anger and the shock etching his bronzed
features into rigidity and she could not bear the sight.
If he turned from her now he would never come back
to her again. She knew that as clearly as though he had
spoken and she fought it with her instincts, reaching up,
touching his sensual mouth with the soft promise of hers,
refusing to let him go.

'Rico...'

And it was done. In the circle of her arms he trembled,
far less in control than he had sought to pretend. His
rigidity broke, his body surging against hers again in a
rhythm as old and as relentless as time. With a stifled

groan of earthy satisfaction he completed his possession of that place which had once been hers alone.

The pain had gone as though it had never been. Renewed heat flooded her as he thrust into her again, fast and deep, his hands sinking beneath her hips to press back her thighs. She gasped as he moved inside her and enforced the pace to a level of shattering, driving intensity. Her heartbeat thundered, her pulses madly accelerated. She was controlled, dominated, excited to a pitch beyond her belief. When she went over the edge into the tumultuous, shuddering pleasure of release she cried out his name as if it were a talisman in the swirling darkness that blocked out everything else in the world.

Except his withdrawal. It could not block out that. Within seconds of that climax Rico dragged himself free of her arms. The shock of that abrupt severance was immense. Bella opened dazed eyes and focused on him. 'What's wrong?'

'*Qué pasa*? "What's wrong?"' Rico sliced the repetition back at her with stinging derision. 'You dare to ask me what's wrong?'

It was like a bucket of cold water on sunburn. Bella sat up, every lingering and pleasurable sensation stolen from her. With a shaking hand she drew the blanket over her. But Rico stood there, unashamedly naked, every taut line of his magnificently masculine body exuding fury.

She had never felt more agonisingly confused. She would not have given herself without love. And with the people she loved Bella was a giver of unparalleled generosity. She asked for nothing in return. But *did* she love him?

'I don't know what's wrong.' She couldn't yet think straight and opted for honesty, searching his hard, dark features with a pain concealed by the veil of her lashes.

'What's your game? What do you want from me? What was that sweet little seduction scene angled at?'

he demanded with raw hostility. 'Had I known I was to be the first I would not have touched you!'

'I think that was my choice to make,' Bella muttered, lowering her head, the sting of tears furiously blinked back.

'*Por Dios* ... it was certainly not mine! I believed I was making love to an equal partner. I do not sleep with virgins,' he said darkly, with a positively vicious bite.

'I told you I was—'

'But you were aware that I did not believe you. If there's one thing you don't look it's *innocent*!' he condemned. 'And innocent in thought and deed you're not. Tell me now ... what is this likely to cost me?'

'C-*cost* you?' she repeated blankly.

'The honey trap and then the price,' he drawled with chilling menace. 'I've been down that path before. This scenario has a deeply sordid familiarity for me. If you're the fertile type I expect I'll be supporting you for the next decade and a half at the very least!'

Every icy word fell like a whiplash on her exposed back. Bella was appalled. He had made love to her with incredible passion, and now he was rejecting both that passion and her with a brutality that paralysed her. 'Rico ...?'

'I warn you now ... I will not marry you,' he imparted with icy emphasis. 'I will never marry again.'

Again? He had already been married? Even in the midst of her turmoil Bella was struck by that unexpected revelation.

'So, if you are cherishing some pitiful fantasy of Cinderella catching her prince, let me assure you that even a pregnancy wouldn't persuade me to make that ultimate sacrifice!'

Bella sucked in badly needed air to fill her seemingly squashed lungs. She studied her tightly clenched hands. 'You're not my prince, Rico. Relax,' she whispered painfully. 'Learn to enjoy life as the toad who didn't deserve to be kissed and transformed. This particular Cinderella doesn't believe in fairy tales.'

He expelled his breath in an audible hiss. She sensed that whatever he had expected from her it hadn't been that. In that sense they were equal. She had been thrown violently off balance by his accusations. Where she had given, he saw deliberate enticement. Where she had expected nothing, he demanded to know the cost. It was impossible to believe that mere minutes ago they had been as intimately close as a man and a woman could be. For when Bella had trustingly dropped all her defences Rico had raised his with a savage hostility which took her breath away. And her pride revolted against the image he had formed of her.

'Why, then? Why did you give yourself to me?'

In a sudden movement Bella scrabbled for her clothes where they lay about the bed. A deep, sustaining anger made her hands tremble. Well, you lived and you learnt. There was no surer truth, it seemed. She had been a fool to expose herself to such an extent to a male who understood her about as well as he might understand an alien being. Where emotions were concerned she was dealing with a male so impenetrably thick that he ought to be locked up for his own safety, she thought furiously.

'Bella...?' he pressed harshly.

'I wanted you! Lust...what else?' Magnificent green eyes flashing, she shot him a look of vibrant derision, unperturbed by his sudden stillness and the freezing of his strong features. 'There was no hidden agenda.'

He stared at her, forbidding dark eyes, fringed by lush ebony lashes, nailed to her with mesmeric intensity. His sensual mouth compressed into a cold, hard line.

'I thought that might shut you up.' Bella let loose a not quite steady laugh as she pulled on her jacket and rummaged beneath the blanket to haul up her skirt. 'Lust is OK for you but not for me, right? Did you think I was about to delicately beat about the bush like your

fancy lady-friends?' she hissed. 'Or did you fondly imagine that I was going to tell you I had fallen madly in
love with you and just couldn't help myself? Get real,
Rico!'

With that final, ringing statement Bella sprang out of
bed and strode through the beaded curtain. She turned
on the water full force at the sink and leant back against
the door, trembling on legs that briefly didn't feel strong
enough to keep her upright. Love grabs you by the throat
when you least expect it and rips the heart out of you,
she thought sickly. I don't *want* this...I don't *need* these
feelings!

Stripping off, she began to wash the scent of him off
her body with slow deliberation. It had been a mistake
and she wasn't too proud to admit to mistakes. Sometimes you played and you lost. Sometimes you made a
fool of yourself. That was life. But as long as you hung
on to your pride and your integrity you would recover.
That was life too.

A knock sounded on the door. Bella said something
very rude and was then ashamed of herself. The use of
bad language was childishly offensive. But, for the first
time in a lot of years, her thoughts and emotions were
in real chaos. She hurt. The shock of that pain sliced
through her, sharp, piercing and inescapable. She had
only to think of the manner in which she had thrown
herself at him and she felt sick with humiliation.

Rico and she didn't fit, didn't suit in any way. They
lived in different worlds. Had fate been kind they would
never even have met. They didn't have a thing in
common. Rico was an ambitious, ruthless, fully paid-
up member of the workaholic financial fraternity. He
didn't have a creative bone in his body.

For heaven's sake, this was a guy who wore pinstriped
suits, kept his desk tidy, thought of precautions against
pregnancy in the midst of stormy passion! He main-
tained a rigorous leash on every spontaneous impulse.

Her virginity had not been a gift, it had been a threat to him! How could she possibly think that she had fallen in love with someone like that? She studied herself, wide-eyed, in the mirror, searching for signs of incipient insanity.

Where had her intelligence gone over the past hour? *Of course* it wasn't love! Their imprisonment had twisted and confused her emotional responses, magnifying them into something they were not. When those bullets had hit the container she had been terrified and Rico had been protective. The release from that terrible tension had sent her emotions into overload. He had offered her comfort and warmth and she had been so grateful for his presence and in such mental turmoil that she had wildly misinterpreted her own feelings.

Really, Bella . . . is that why you recklessly gave away the virginity you were saving for your future husband? She paled, crushing that inner voice. But right through her teens Bella had been indoctrinated by her grand-father's moral standards. It had been an education. Cleo had had an 'anything goes' outlook on the morality front. But her lifestyle hadn't made her happy.

Bitterly aware of that reality, Bella had decided that the field of sexual experimentation was not for her. If she loved someone and he loved her, and a future together was on the cards, that would have been dif-ferent. But passion without love . . . That had been the biggest 'do not' in Bella's rulebook. And she had just broken that rule. Received her just deserts in record time too, she acknowledged on another wave of pain.

Rico had illuminated another light when she emerged. What had happened to conservation? she wondered nastily. But then she saw him standing in the shadows by the curtain and her ability to be sharp and critical momentarily deserted her. She was assailed by a blinding urge to rush back into his arms and that terrified her. It was as though there were two people inside her—one trying to be sensible, one racing out of control on an emotional roller coaster. What the heck was the matter with her? Rico looked as dangerous as a prowling predator and she had already found out the hard way that she bled when he clawed.

'I believe that I have misjudged you,' he conceded in his silky, accented drawl which trickled down her sensitive spinal column like the caress of rich velvet.

'Forget it. I already have.' But her nervous antenna went on to instant red alert.

The level of physical awareness splintering through the atmosphere between them shattered her. Instead of fading with satiation, as she had naïvely assumed they would, the sexual vibrations had merely intensified. Bella went into restive retreat. She turned away to the fridge, her skin heating, her brain suddenly a wasteland awash with a devastating wave of unbelievably unwelcome erotic imagery. Her body ached and burned with the memory of that wild passion.

'Lust works for me as well,' Rico murmured in a purring undertone.

Her lashes fluttered. She froze halfway into the fridge, certain that he couldn't have said that. 'I don't want to talk about it,' she mumbled, intimate recollection having vanquished her defences.

'Don't be coy, *gatita*. It doesn't suit you.'

Her cheeks burning fierily, Bella straightened. 'Look, I made a mistake, and not one I intend to repeat . . .' She had forced herself to look at him and her voice trailed away as she registered that his attention was no longer directed at her.

Reaching for the light, Rico took an abrupt stride forward and held it above the stove, his glittering gaze fixed on some point above her. '*Infierno!*' he breathed.

Dazedly Bella watched him set aside the light at speed and reach up to touch the surface of the roof round the metal flue of the chimney. 'What is it?' she demanded.

'Get me the poker!'

'But—?' Meeting the whiplash effect of his impatience, Bella moved to oblige.

Grasping the poker, he swung it up against the roof. A piece of something like plaster or cement broke away and fell to the floor. 'What are you doing?' she gasped.

But as he struck the roof again and more debris flew down, sending up a cloud of dust which made her cough, she realised exactly what he was doing. When the flue for the stove had been put in a hole had naturally been cut and, for simplicity's sake, not a circular one. A rectangle of metal had been removed. She could dimly see the edges exposed and her momentary excitement faded.

'They welded it back in after cutting it to take the flue.'

'That isn't steel!' Rico gritted. 'And it's only spot-welded. It'll come out!'

With punishing force he rammed the poker up against the insert, which buckled under the blow. Her heart in her mouth, Bella watched him batter it until it came loose, and then plant two powerful hands round the flue. The upper section lifted away and dim light filtered in. With a powerful push Rico rammed the section upwards, slamming it out onto the roof to clear the aperture he had exposed.

Bella's fingernails, which had been biting into her palms, bit even harder. Acid tears hit the back of her eyes as she looked up. 'It isn't big enough to take either of us!'

Rico surveyed her with raw determination. 'With a little help from me it'll take you,' he asserted.

Awkwardly she climbed up onto the top of the stove and raised her head through the aperture, her eyes flying up and down and around the rafters, the sheet-iron roof above the rusting hulk of an old tractor lying in the corner. 'We're in a barn,' she whispered.

'*Santa María*!' Rico slashed from below her in raw disbelief. 'You're not up there to see the scenery!'

Before she could react a pair of hands closed round her thighs and forced her upwards, not even giving her time to hunch her shoulders. Her collision with the edges of the rough metal hurt and she uttered a stifled shriek to which he paid no attention at all. He simply lifted her again, and this time she automatically curved her shoulders in and she went through, snaking out her hands to brace herself in amazement on the roof. With his help she hauled herself through the rest of the way.

'Now get me out of here!' Rico urged from below, as if he was afraid that she might go off and paint her nails or something and forget about him.

Her heart thudding like a wild creature's, perspiration beading her upper lip, she lowered herself down off the roof, hitting the rough ground below hard enough to jar her ankle-bones painfully. In a stumbling run she raced round to the doors. If they were locked—dear God, if they were locked . . .

For the next few frantic minutes it crossed her mind more than once that they might as well have been as she pushed and hauled and thrust with all her might, sweat rolling off her as she struggled to drive back the bolts, and all the time Rico was shouting at her from inside.

'Shut up!' she screamed, pausing to get her breath back.

It took her another ten minutes and he didn't shut up. As the bolts finally gave that final, necessary inch Bella slumped back winded on the dirty ground, as wrung out as a limp dish rag. Rico strode out and the first thing he did, which she found quite inconceivable, was to close the doors again and force the bolts back with an ease that made her hate him.

With a powerful hand he hauled her upright and dragged her towards the rickety barn doors.

'Suppose *they* are out there?' she hissed.

Rico, his dark features alight with savage determination, shot her a silencing glance. He pushed the barn door back slowly and she tried to duck under his arm to see what was beyond. Rain was lashing down in sheets outside.

'Come on ... skulking here isn't going to get us anywhere,' he asserted.

She sidled out after him, paradoxically appalled by the emptiness she saw all around them. A derelict stone cottage lay off to one side, and in every other direction all she could see was the rough moorland edging the muddy track that ran down the hill. There was no sign of life anywhere.

'Now what?'

The wind and the rain made a truly ghastly combination as they raced down the lane. Rico hauled her relentlessly in his wake and she forced herself onward, fearfully aware that they were not safe until they could transport themselves some distance from their prison. They reached a road, not a very wide one—the sort of road which might see a vehicle maybe once a day, she thought hysterically.

'I'm so cold,' she gasped, soaked to the skin and shivering.

'Moving will keep you warm.' Shimmering dark eyes appraised her. His mouth tightened. He wrenched off his jacket and held it out to her.

Bella gave him a startled glance before she dug her numbed arms into the sleeves. 'Now *you'll* freeze,' she muttered guiltily.

'The subtle difference between a creep and a gentleman—the creep stays warm,' he drawled from between clenched teeth. 'We have to find shelter. It'll be dark soon.'

The road twisted and curved downhill for what felt like miles, and at the foot of that hill met yet another narrow road. Without any other options they kept on

heading down. The rain slackened off but both of them
were so wet that it made little difference. When they
finally rounded a corner and saw a dim light at the top
of a rough track Bella thought it was a mirage. Every
muscle in her body ached by that stage and her steps
were clumsy and wildly uncoordinated. Even speaking
was too much of an effort. She stopped, staggering like
a drunk.

Rico put a strong arm around her and propelled her
towards the track. Later she couldn't recall climbing that
final hill. A dog circled them, barking fit to wake the
dead. A light went on, blinding her, and she came to a
halt and swayed.

'Come on,' Rico pressed, and he was already almost
carrying her.

She tried—she really did try—but in all her life she
had never been so tired. Her legs simply folded beneath
her, her head swimming, and she sank down into the
thick, welcoming darkness behind her eyelids without a
murmur.

'Wake up...'

Bella surfaced, cocooned in wonderful warmth, a
fleecy blanket against her cheek. Her eyes opened and
focused on the logs crackling in the grate several feet
from her, and then landed on Rico, who had crouched
down to block her view of the fire. She searched his
starkly handsome features with softened green eyes. A
helpless smile curved her lips.

'You look wonderful.' Her voice was slurred, sounding
as though it was coming from miles away, and with immense effort she freed a hand from the blanket and
reached out to him, curving her palm against his blue-
shadowed jaw-line. 'But you need a shave.'

'*Muchas gracias, querida mia.*' She connected with his
brilliant golden eyes and her heart turned right over. He
caught her hand in his and pressed his mouth almos⁺

reverentially to the centre of her palm. 'You scared me,' he muttered roughly.

He sprang upright again and moved out of her view. It was still too much of an effort to turn her head. She heard another voice, female, elderly, somewhere behind her. Rico said something about a phone, and the lady was talking nineteen to the dozen about food and hot baths and him needing to change out of his clothes *right this minute*, stressing the fact with the kind of gentle but steely authority which reminded Bella very much of one of her former schoolteachers.

She drifted off again then, curiously uninterested in her unfamiliar surroundings, content merely with the warmth and the feeling of security. Time had no meaning until Rico reappeared. He bent down and swept her up off the sofa. 'You can have a bath now that you have warmed up sufficiently,' he informed her.

That struck Bella as hilariously funny. She giggled.

'By the sound of it you're feeling better.' An elderly woman with a stern but smiling face looked down at her where she lay nestled in perfect relaxation against Rico's broad chest. 'Some day you'll be able to tell your grandchildren that you almost died of exposure on your honeymoon. That should provoke a few interesting questions.'

'Honeymoon?' Bella whispered blankly as Rico carried her up a flight of stairs.

He set her down on a chair in a large, old-fashioned bathroom and peeled her out of the blanket. She was dismayed to discover that she was wearing not a stitch of clothing, but before she could react to the startling discovery he had lifted her up and settled her down into a massive Victorian bath filled with deliciously hot water.

'Honeymoon?' she said again.

'I thought it best not to tell the truth. I said that we had got lost and our car had broken down. Mrs Warwick is a widow living alone. This is a remote place. I wished to minimise any fears she might have about opening her doors so generously and trustingly to complete strangers who look far from respectable.' As he talked he was stripping off his clothes.

Bella's cheeks warmed to a temperature that had little to do with the bath water. Smooth brown shoulders gave way to a muscular torso sprinkled with curling black hair that arrowed down into an intriguingly silky furrow over his flat stomach and then... Embarrassed, she glanced away, but still she saw him before her—the lean, angular hips, the long, powerful thighs, the sleeping promise of his manhood in a nest of ebony curls.

'You were wearing a ring on your right hand. When I was undressing you downstairs I slid it onto your wedding finger.'

Belatedly she noticed the ring. 'It was my grandmother's.'

'Move over...'

'*Rico*!' Bella twisted her head round and skidded forward towards the taps in a rush, water sloshing noisily everywhere as he simply stepped into the bath behind her. 'Lord, you're cold!' she gasped, all of a quiver as a pair of long, icy thighs closed round her hips from behind. 'Sorry, I should've thought. I'll get out!'

As she began to get up he reached for her and pulled her back, bringing her down on top of him, anchoring both arms round her. Above her head he laughed sonorously as she went from rigid to trembling and back again. 'You have so much to learn, *gatita mia*. I shall enjoy teaching you.'

Bella squinted frantically down at the hands firmly cupping the pouting thrust of her breasts and blushed. Beneath his palms she could feel her nipples swelling and tightening in shameless, instantaneous response. 'Rico...?'

'I have informed my chief executive, Kenway, of our whereabouts. I also spoke to the police. Thanks to Mrs

Warwick, I was able to give the exact location of the barn,' he imparted with sudden harshness. 'They will stake it out and wait until those bastards come back to check on us again. They will walk into a trap just as we did in that car park. The police will be waiting for them.'

The icy chill in his voice made her shiver. All Bella had thought about was freedom—the luxury of the fire and the bath, the wonderful release from fear to *safety*. Her world had not yet expanded beyond those things. The intensity of her relief and her continuing exhaustion had combined to blunt and blur her reasoning powers. Rico, she noted, was not similarly affected. He was already grimly anticipating their kidnappers' capture and punishment.

'Had they asked for a ransom?'

'*Sì*...and the agreed arrangements will continue so that they do not become suspicious. Kenway has been in constant touch with Hector Barsay on your behalf. He will inform him of your release—'

'How did they know who I was?' A yawn was creeping up on her. She was lying naked in a bath with a man and she was ready to fall asleep, so complete was her relaxation. She couldn't believe it.

'My chauffeur knew your address,' he reminded her. 'Had he not, the police might have suspected that you had something to do with the kidnapping.'

'Me?' It barely penetrated. Her eyelids felt as if someone had attached weights to them, but she wasn't so far gone that she was not aware that Rico's lean, hard length was reacting far more energetically to her proximity. But she didn't tense, only smiled sleepily. There was something so wonderfully reassuring about being that close to Rico.

'You're falling asleep,' he groaned with more than a hint of incredulity.

She wanted to remind him that she had been up since half past four in the morning, battering doors, posting 'help' notes through the container roof, while he had slept until noon, but she couldn't find the energy. And he seemed to understand for he sat up and pulled her with him, and a minute later she was wrapped in a fleecy towel. Like a child she stood there, dead on her feet, while he patted her dry and pulled something over her head— something crisp and cotton and clean-smelling.

And then she was sinking into a warm bed without even caring how she had got there, sighing with pleasure as every limb relaxed. Voices spoke over her head. The smell of food briefly flared her nostrils but even that couldn't push back the sleep enclosing her.

In the darkness, a long time later, Bella shifted against a warm, hard body and curved instinctively closer, her hand splaying over a hair-roughened chest, her cheek resting against a smooth shoulder. 'Rico,' she breathed sleepily in instant recognition combined with instant contentment, and she would have drifted away again had he not tangled a hand in the mane of her tumbled hair, tipped her mouth up and kissed her.

It was like coming alive when you thought you were dead. Every skin-cell suddenly flamed into red-hot life, a kind of frantic, feverish hunger possessing her. Her response was so intense that it swallowed her alive.

'Rico...' She gasped again as he pinned her to the mattress beneath him and kissed her breathless, his mouth, hard, hungry, hot, exciting her beyond bearing.

He freed her and wrenched the nightdress off. In the darkness there was no warning before his mouth closed round the engorged bud of one swelling breast. The sensation hit her with stunning effect. Her neck extended in an arch, a stifled moan torn from her when she felt the erotic brush of his teeth and his tongue as he pulled on her taut nipples. And there was no time for anything, not a single thought, nothing but the raw, driving intensity of need screaming through her veins.

His lips skimmed a tormenting path over the quivering muscles of her belly, his hands parting her thighs, and then he was doing something ... something so intimate that she tensed in sudden alarm before the power of simple sensation tore her every inhibition away. And then she was lost again in a hot, swirling fire, conscious of nothing but the incredible, torturous excitement roaring mindlessly out of her control as he employed the same technique on the most sensitive flesh of all.

She was at screaming-point when he moved over her, every shred of physical awareness centred on the ache of emptiness between her thighs. And then he thrust into her and she moaned and arched in one taut movement, her body clenching on a pleasure so intense that she was utterly possessed by it. Her fingers raked down his back in reaction and her teeth nipped at the strong brown column of his throat in instinctive revenge for the ragged laugh he gave vent to.

After that there was nothing but the long, pulsing drive for satisfaction. It went on and on and on. She hit the heights fast, unable to rein back the flood of release, but he didn't stop. She had barely hit ground level again before the frantic climb back up began, and in all her life she had never felt so controlled, never dreamt she could enjoy that reality so much. And when the second climax whooshed up inside her she was wiped out.

He shuddered above her, every muscle clenching taut, and she put her arms round him, happiness flooding through her like a rejuvenating drug. There was only one thought in her mind as she sank back into sleep. She would never let go of him again.

CHAPTER SIX

'SOME more tea, Mrs da Silva?'

Out of the corner of her eye Bella noticed Rico tense just as he had the last time their hostess had addressed her as his wife. 'Please call me Bella,' she said tightly, politely refusing the offer of a refill for her cup.

Rico had wakened her when he was already dressed. That had been her first shock. Shaven, his shirt immaculately clean—thanks, no doubt, to Mrs Warwick's ministrations—his tie reinstated and his exquisitely expensive suit pressed and only a little limp from yesterday's soaking, this was not Rico as she remembered him during their captivity—it was Rico the intimidating international financier she had faced at the bank.

'A car will pick us up at eight. We will make our statements to the police as soon as possible,' he had murmured smoothly before leaving her alone to rise and dress.

Her attention had fallen on the nightgown which had been discarded on the carpet the night before, and suddenly Bella had felt as though she was dying inside. How *could* she have made love with him again? The fevered, driving passion of the night haunted her now. He had a bruise from her teeth a half-inch above his collar and it seemed to scream at her like a badge of public shame every time she looked at him.

In the dark he was one hundred per cent sexual predator and she was one hundred per cent victim of her own wanton nature. Recalling that she had been all over him like a rash afterwards only intensified her sense of humiliation. There was a new distance between them and it wasn't coming from her side of the fence. Rico had an aloof quality that he hadn't had the night before. It had been there from the first moment she'd set eyes on him again.

And she understood, wished she didn't, wished she were wrong, but knew she was right. The *real* world was about to reclaim them again. Their time together in that container had been time outside the real world. Now they were back to being the people they really were. He was Rico da Silva, rich, influential financier... and she was Bella Jennings, an illegitimate waitress who wanted to be an artist but who might never make the grade. The gulf was enormous and Rico had been the first to recall it.

Her inner turmoil was so intense that it threatened to swallow her alive. Suddenly she was wallowing in terrifying confusion, not knowing what she felt, not knowing what she thought. Involuntarily she collided with the dark density of Rico's flashing gaze and her heart stopped beating altogether. Was it possible that he was enduring the same conflict?

But then she watched him smoothly turn his dark head and speak calmly to Mrs Warwick, and her heart beat again and sank simultaneously. Rico was in control. Rico knew exactly what he was thinking and feeling. Confusion and Rico da Silva were not a credible combination. Why had he made love to her again last night? Why had he pounced and moved in when she had been half-asleep, her every defence mechanism at rest?

P for predator, P for passionate, P for prey. Her stomach heaved. He was a very virile male. When he wanted sex he was used to taking it. She had just been a willing female body in the bed and, as he had once reminded her, he was not a corpse, devoid of all sexual response. And if he was now wishing that he hadn't bothered, she had no doubt that he had the cold will to

ensure that she didn't form any silly ideas about their
possibly having embarked on a continuing relationship.

The four-wheel drive that picked them up arrived early,
hastening their departure from the farmhouse. Two men
were seated in front. They hadn't even reached the end
of the lane before she realised that they were policemen
driving an unmarked car—a chief superintendent and
an inspector, no less. The taut questions came flying
within seconds.

Every time a question came in her direction Rico
stepped in to answer it for her. In another mood, in
another situation and with other companions, Bella
would have roundly objected. But right now she felt de-
tached from everything, everybody...Rico and the police
included...and she didn't care—she really didn't care—
if sitting there in silence, letting him do the talking for
her, made her look like the dumbest cluck of all time.

Her mind had already leapt forward to the parting of
the ways ahead. Her thoughts stayed there, frozen in
intense shock at the image of forthcoming loss and departure that unexpectedly tore at her.

'Miss Jennings?' a voice said loudly.

Dredged from her inner conflict, Bella jerked and
flinched, and found herself staring wordlessly at the older
man in the passenger seat, who had turned round and
was studying her intently. 'Sorry, I—'

A hand suddenly closed tightly round hers where it
lay clenched on the seat. 'Bella's still in shock,' Rico
delivered with chilling bite, and 'leave her alone' was
writ large in his assertion.

Shaken by that hand on hers and that cold intonation,
Bella saw the senior policeman's gaze drop and linger
on their linked hands, and abruptly a tide of burning
colour flushed her cheeks. 'I'm fine,' she said tremulously, shielding her eyes with her lashes.

'We do require some form of statement from Miss
Jennings. Of course, I understand what a devastating

experience this must have been.' Even so, there was the merest edge of wry amusement in the older man's voice and she knew then that he knew that, whatever their relationship might have been before they had ended up in that container, it was now one of intimacy, and that stifled her natural effervescence even more. She did *not* want anyone else to be aware of what she could barely deal with herself. She snaked her fingers free of Rico's, denying herself that warmth although every treacherous sense longed to maintain it.

There was a town not many miles from the farmhouse, complete with police station. They were practically smuggled into the building through a rear entrance.

'Can't hold the Press off much longer, though,' the chief superintendent sighed.

'The *Press*?' Bella gasped.

'They'll be down on us like vultures the minute they know we're free,' Rico drawled flatly.

'They could blow the whole bloody show,' the inspector chipped in bitterly as they were hustled into a small, bare interviewing room which made Bella feel more claustrophobic than she had ever felt in the container.

'The Press know about us?' she whispered dazedly.

'We have their agreement to hold off on printing a word, but *now* . . . well, let's say there's a risk of a leak before we get a proper chance at catching those b-blighters.' He selected the word grimly.

'Miss Jennings will be staying at my estate,' Rico volunteered without any expression at all. 'My staff are trustworthy.'

'*Her* story has got to be worth a quarter of a mill flat, even at a conservative estimate,' the inspector muttered with cold cynicism. 'I hope you know what you're doing.'

She heard the senior policeman's slight intake of breath, knew the inspector was all at sea as to what he had said wrong. And several lowering realisations hit

Bella very hard all at once. The police *already* knew all
about her—her background, the accident through which
she had met Rico, her unarguable poverty. Even as a
victim she had been investigated, possibly just to make
sure that she was *indeed* a victim... Rico's remark in
the bath the previous night—about her being a suspect—
returned to haunt her.

And clearly in the inspector's biased view she was
exactly the kind of woman who was likely to jump on
some tabloid bandwagon and tell all for a price.

'Bella's not going to talk.'

Glancing up, she met Rico's brilliant golden gaze,
aimed at her like a stranglehold and a gag. That look
spoke not of faith but of threat. If you talk I'll personally throttle you, that look said. Her cup of humiliation ran right over there and then. She looked away,
her facial muscles locking tight, an acrid sting burning
her eyelids. 'O ye of little faith', she reflected, in more
pain than she could have believed possible and sick to
the heart from it.

Did he really think that he was in danger of waking
up some morning soon to a kiss-and-tell revelation about
their lovemaking in captivity? Her stomach churned.
After all they had gone through together he still dis-
trusted her. So maybe she wasn't a whore, but she could
still be a greedy little gold-digger, it seemed! And *this*
was the male that every hateful instinct urged her to cling
to and stay with?

That was when she knew it was over between them—
absolutely, finally and conclusively over, regardless of
what she did or did not feel for Rico da Silva.

'Of course she's not about to talk.' The older
policeman patted her shoulder in reassurance as he tact-
fully angled her down into a chair, and she had the bitter
pleasure of appreciating that a man who had met her
only an hour ago already knew and understood more
about her than Rico did.

She answered questions like an automaton. Inside herself she just wanted to die behind her forced smiles, but torture wouldn't have wrung an ounce of her true feelings from her. Pride... Thank the Lord it was there for her when she most needed it. Rico watched her like a hawk throughout, as if he were programmed to probe that uncharacteristic complete emotional withdrawal of hers. But she really didn't credit him with that much sensitivity.

The noisy clatter of rotor blades stole through her self-imposed inner wall, her darkened green eyes briefly revealing her turmoil as she frowned.

'Mr da Silva's helicopter landing in the car park,' the chief super revealed. 'I'll take you wherever you want to go, Miss Jennings. I'm heading back to London.'

'Bella's coming with me,' Rico murmured drily without a single shade of doubt.

Without looking at him, so grateful to the older man that she could have grabbed his hand and kissed it, Bella sprang upright. 'Thanks, but I have friends I can go to... friends I want to be with,' she muttered abruptly.

'Perhaps you could leave us alone for a moment?' Rico suggested smoothly to their companions.

'I'll be waiting outside,' the chief super told her, with a wry smile. And then the door closed, sealing them into the privacy which she would have done any craven thing to avoid, but which her intelligence told her had to be faced.

'What the hell are you playing at?' Rico enquired harshly. 'Of course you're coming with me!'

She had to force herself to look at him again. She had to know, before she walked away, that she was making the only possible decision... and yet she already knew that, and loathed herself for being weak enough to require further proof. 'I'm not going to talk to the Press,' she said stiffly.

The faintest hint of dark colour accentuated the angular slant of his hard cheekbones. His hooded dark eyes were nailed to her, however, without any perceptible emotion at all. He made no comment on her reassurance. His sensual mouth twisted. 'I want you to come with me.'

'Why? The party's over... don't you think?' Behind her mocking grin she felt like somebody handing a murderer a knife.

'But I don't mind if the band plays on... for a while,' he murmured, coolly careful to conclude with that candour.

He had used the knife without compunction. It was sex, nothing else. That was all he wanted—a temporary affair in the privacy of his home, with the added security of knowing that she couldn't talk to the Press while he was around. Neat, tidy, every necessity covered, sexual and otherwise... so much Rico's stamp that she wanted to shout and scream and claw him.

But she didn't. She used her talons to hang on like grim death to her pride instead. 'I don't think so.' Turning, unable to meet his sharp appraisal any longer, she began moving towards the door.

'You're as hot for me as I am for you, *gatita*... and I won't make you a better offer,' he warned with silken insolence.

Her spine stiffened. She spun back, unable to let that go unchallenged. 'So what? You think that matters to me?' she demanded shakily.

'I want you in my bed.' The admission might have been wrenched by force from him. His strong face was hard and taut, his eyes as dark as black ice, biting into her almost accusingly.

Bella gave vent to an edgy laugh. 'I'm sure you've got no shortage of willing replacements!'

'And what if you're pregnant?'

Bella paled but her magnificent eyes flashed at him. 'Highly unlikely...it was the wrong time,' she told him brittlely as she made for the door again, really desperate this time to escape.

'Then allow me.' He reached the door ahead of her and swung it wide. 'Look after yourself,' he murmured drily as she preceded him into the corridor. And then he was gone, striding past her in the direction of the rear exit.

On cotton-wool legs she wandered down to the window and stood there, watching him walk out and spring into the waiting helicopter. Well, that was that, she told herself. The feeling that she had been cut in half without an anaesthetic would wear off. She was not, could not be, in love with a creep like that. Fear had somehow made her emotions centre on him. She had become disgustingly dependent, weak and vulnerable, but now that the whole ghastly experience was over she would swiftly recover and return to normal.

'A self-contained bastard, isn't he?'

Her head flipped round, her every feeling exposed. And the chief super placed a supportive arm round her and wafted her out to his car. He asked her where she wanted to go and then handed her a box of tissues. Sorry, he had four adult daughters, he told her ruefully; couldn't help reading her like a book. He had seen her paintings, he told her. Fabulous, out of this world, he added almost shyly. Was there the slightest chance that she would sell one?

And that cracked her shell as nothing else could have done. The tears flooded out, and she got dug into the tissues with the agonised acknowledgement that this stranger, this kind, clever man whom she barely knew, knew so much more about her than the arrogant, hateful swine she had stupidly, recklessly gone to bed with!

It was a long drive down to Liz's country cottage. With Liz she knew she was always welcome and she knew that

Liz would keep her mouth shut. And she even knew where her friend kept her spare key—under the second tub of pansies to the left of the back door. The policeman was appalled, but to her he didn't feel like a policeman any more. He had become Maurice during the drive.

'I'll stay until your friend gets home,' he told her.

'I want to be on my own.'

He studied her and then sighed. 'If he asks where—?'

'No!' she interrupted, with helpless force.

'I'll keep you in touch with developments,' he asserted, and took his leave with a touching reluctance to leave her alone.

Liz wouldn't be back until far later than she had admitted to him. This was her night with the art club. She dined in town those nights and went straight to the college for her class. Liz was an accountant, several years Bella's senior, who painted great, vibrant canvases of the flowers she loved and enjoyed a lucrative sideline from their sales. She joked that her clients would be unnerved by that flamboyant side to her nature and only ever signed her creations with her initials.

Gramps had enrolled Bella in the art club long before she'd attended art college at seventeen. She had been the youngest in the class and had had no training whatsoever, but from her first visit the instructor had been excited by what he'd called her 'raw talent'. More worried than pleased by his enthusiasm, her grandfather had got in touch with Hector through the medium of one of Cleo's fleeting visits. It had been Hector who had advised them on what art college and which course, Hector who had taken charge of her artistic development.

She made a dive for Liz's phone, suddenly desperate to hear Hector's querulous but familiar voice.

'I was worried sick when those nosy policemen landed on the doorstep,' he complained furiously, making her smile. 'And I don't want any blasted reporters following them!'

'I'll stay here until the fuss blows over. I'll ring the restaurant and tell them I'm sick,' she muttered, speaking her thoughts out loud on the subject of her job.

'That Griff character has been calling too. Give him a ring,' Hector advised irritably, and then added as an afterthought, 'You didn't damage your hands, did you?'

'Just my heart.'

'I beg your pardon?'

'Never mind. I'll keep in touch.'

'Phone calls cost a fortune,' he reminded her in dismay. 'The Royal Mail is expensive but considerably cheaper in comparison.'

She came off the phone and laughed until she cried. Through her tears she picked up Liz's sketch-pad and began to draw, her agile fingers moving at speed over the paper. Only when she registered what she was drawing did she stop. With a choking sensation in her throat she looked down sickly at the slashing lines of Rico's impassive face as she had last seen him.

She threw the pad aside, in more turmoil than ever. She would work through this, get her feet pinned back down hard to ground level and gather her common sense if it killed her! After all, a week ago she hadn't even known Rico da Silva walked the same earth. But he *didn't*, she reflected with sudden fierce anger; he didn't walk the same earth at all.

'I feel like an idiot... a total, absolute idiot!' Griff complained for the third time. 'Every one of my partners is sniggering behind his hands. So what *did* happen in that blasted container between the two of you? I have a right to know!'

'The same way I have the right to know who was with you the night of my birthday?' As soon as she said it she regretted it. Griff was very handsome but suddenly, betrayed by his fair skin, he looked like a guilty beetroot that had been stabbed unexpectedly in the back by a pickle fork.

'Well, I . . . I don't know what you're talking about! I was working that night.'

He lied so badly that she was embarrassed for him. Why was he being so possessive all of a sudden? Why was it that even an unfaithful man suddenly hung on like grim death when he sensed that you were ready to break it off? It crossed her mind that Rico hadn't hung on...Rico had been off like an Olympic sprinter... Only good manners had made him let her out of the door in front of him.

'OK.' Griff heaved a constricted sigh. 'Guilty...but it was only a flirtation... I was tempted, that's all. Unforgivable, I know, on your birthday—'

'Don't you think that date was subconsciously chosen to hurt most?'

He looked blankly back at her. She was too clever for him, could practically tell him what he was about to say before he parted his lips, and whatever had been between them had evaporated entirely on her side. She decided to let him off the hook.

'Look, it doesn't matter, does it? We're finished. Good *friends* still, I hope,' she stressed gently. 'But that's all, Griff.'

'I didn't sleep with her!' He startled her by surging across Liz's tiny lounge with an amount of emotion she would never have expected from a male usually so cool and controlled. 'And I'm sorry; I'll never do it again,' he swore, grasping both her hands.

He *had* slept with that other woman. She could tell, but it was not her place, after what had happened with Rico, to stand in pious judgement.

'Let's go out to dinner somewhere very public,' he urged tautly. 'You have to come out of hiding some time. Da Silva's "no comment" is beginning to fall pretty hard

on my ears! You're my girlfriend, for God's sake, but
all that trash in the tabloids and your disappearance is
giving everyone the idea...well, that you've got something to be ashamed of!'

Liz walked into the tiny bedroom where she was
changing. 'You're going *out* with him?'

'It seems that I owe it to him to help him save face
with his colleagues in the office.'

'He never said that, surely?'

'I don't think he even realises that that is what he said.
I'll pack. It's time I went home anyway.' A rueful smile
curved Bella's lips. 'Thanks for having me, but I've got
to face the music sooner or later. Not that I'm expecting
to be mobbed. I'm old news since our kidnappers were
caught. There won't be much interest now until the case
reaches court,' she pointed out.

'Don't you believe it... You've got a price on your
head whether you like it or not! And the longer you
keep quiet about your *ordeal*,' Liz said grimly, 'the more
outrageous become the tabloid fantasies. You'd be better
off issuing a statement.'

Bella sat silently in Griff's BMW as it transported her
back to London. The more questions he asked about
Rico the tenser she became. Why the heck couldn't he
just take the hint and shut up?

It had been three weeks since she had been dropped
by the chief superintendent at her friend's cottage.
Hector had packed a case for her and Liz had collected
it covertly from his back door, because the Press had
been encamped at the front continuously during those
first days after her captors' arrest. She had twice been
collected and smuggled into a central London police
station where the evidence against their kidnappers was
being carefully stockpiled. But all that was over, bar the
court case.

Only now did she wonder if it would ever be over. The Press had ferreted into her past and published *everything*—her colourful parentage, her cursory education, her artistic talent. It seemed to her that everyone she had ever known in life had talked about her to the tabloids—Gramps' neighbours, fellow students at the college, her tutor, former boyfriends—bitter and otherwise. 'Frigid', had said one; 'wild', had said another. I'M STILL IN LOVE WITH HER, had screamed the headline given by an ex she barely recalled from six months ago.

She didn't recognize the *femme fatale* the tabloids had depicted her as. Her every piece of privacy had been ripped from her resistant body. She had been invaded, raped in print and twisted into something she was not, and as far as she could see there was not a damn thing she could do about it!

'*Here*?' Bella gasped when she realised where Griff was planning that they should dine. 'You'll be broke for six months!'

'Will you keep your voice down?' he hissed at her, paling to the same shade as his brand-new dinner jacket. 'I can well afford to splash out occasionally.'

Only he had never splashed out for her benefit before. Griff might have earned a very healthy crust as a partner in a busy legal firm but he was careful with his cash. Was he celebrating something—a more than usually lucrative divorce?

The head waiter looked at her with recognition. She threw her slim shoulders back and smoothed her elbow-high black gloves up her arms. Her figure-hugging black velvet dress could mercifully hold its own in any company. A seventies designer original, the colour spectacular against her wealth of vibrant Titian hair and creamy skin, its deceptively simple cut made the most of her lithe, female shape and fabulous legs.

Their table was right in the very centre of the crowded dining room. 'Are we celebrating something?' Bella whispered, maddeningly conscious of heads turning in their direction. Surely not all these beautiful people read the same rubbishy tabloids?

'I hope so.' Griff gave her a wide, self-satisfied smile as their menus arrived and he ordered wine in execrable French.

'I don't drink,' she reminded him.

He leant almost confidingly closer. 'I believe you'll break that rule tonight.'

Just as she was on the brink of questioning the peculiarity of his behaviour, Bella's attention was stolen. Griff could have stood up and stripped and she wouldn't have noticed. Rico da Silva was in the act of taking a seat at a table about fifteen feet away. She froze, her heartbeat slowing to a dulled thud as if she was being forced to witness a disaster. And, inside herself, indeed she was...

For three endless weeks Bella had rationalised away every single feeling that Rico had inspired in her. She had blamed fear, propinquity, hysteria and her own repressed sexuality. She had lost weight, endured sleepless nights and stubbornly considered herself cured of emotions that she refused to rate higher than the level of an adolescent infatuation.

But at the same second as her shocked gaze located him and everyone else in the room vanished from her awareness, her so-called cure came apart at the seams. A hunger so intense that it was agonising clawed at her. Her mesmerised eyes roved from his dark head to the soles of his hand-made shoes and back up again. Worst of all, she couldn't stop herself from doing it.

'Your wine...' Griff prodded her fingers with the glass at the same instant as Rico's dark, restive gaze landed on her. Bella watched his hard, bronzed face tauten with something that looked very much like savage disbelief, and hurriedly she tore her dazed scrutiny from him. She fumbled for the wine and drank the whole glass down in one go.

'I do realise that you haven't indulged before,' Griff reproved, 'but one is supposed to enjoy the bouquet.'

The waiter was already refilling her glass.

'Now...' Griff dealt her an expectant look.

'Now what?'

Belatedly she noticed the ring glittering in the palm which he was extending to her. 'What do you want me to do with that?' she muttered helplessly.

'I am asking you to marry me,' he told her smugly, reaching for her hand.

'You're what?'

Everything happened at once. A camera flash went off somewhere near by. The head waiter looked shattered. A man in a dinner jacket, clasping a camera, raced past... 'Thanks mate!' he tossed back, apparently at Griff, as he headed for the exit fast.

'I'm sure you won't mind if we join you.'

Open-mouthed, Bella stared incredulously as Rico, appearing out of nowhere, cooly pulled out one of the two vacant chairs at their table for the exquisite blonde who was hovering with an air of unease beside him.

'Sophie Ingram, this is Bella. Bella, meet Sophie. Since we are the cynosure for every eye in the room, we might as well join up, *es verdad*?'

'*Es verdad* nothing!' Bella hissed, recovering her tongue. 'I do not wish to share a table with you. You're butting in where you are not wanted—'

'Bella, *please*,' Griff intervened in a shocked whisper.

'If you whisper at Bella you'll make her shout,' Rico murmured flatly, sinking down into the seat beside her and signalling to the hovering head waiter with an imperious movement of one hand. 'Now, you are Griff Atherton... Does she accidentally call you Biff from time to time? I ask because when we first met it took Bella four attempts to even recall my name.'

'Shut up!' she bit out from between clenched teeth.

'Bella, please,' Griff said again. 'Mr da Silva and Miss Ingram are very welcome.'

'Of course we're welcome,' Rico drawled with lancing satire, shooting Griff a look of unconcealed derision.

Bella reached for her glass and drained it for a second time all in one go.

'I'm very sorry about this,' Sophie murmured, openly studying the engagement ring still lying on the linen cloth in front of Bella.

'Wedding bells...' Rico laughed sardonically.

'If you don't shut up and back off,' Bella spat in a shaking undertone, 'I'm going to hit you with that bottle!'

'That would be a first.' Incandescent golden eyes challenged her, his strong mouth twisting. 'Another first. But not one half as enjoyable as the last we shared.'

'Excuse me.' It took immense restraint but Bella shakily reached for her bag and rose from the table.

She reached the cloackroom only seconds before Sophie. She spun from the sink her green eyes swimming with tears. The blonde gave her a wry glance. 'If I could do to Rico what you can do, I wouldn't be crying over it.'

'I don't know what you're talking about,' Bella said in a stifled voice.

'You're so young.' Sophie sighed, studying her averted profile. 'I came to bitch but I can't. It isn't your fault he's about to dump me—he never stays with anyone longer than a couple of months. I'm past my sell-by date and frankly I've had enough. Rico has been like a stranger since the kidnapping—'

'Has he?' Bella looked up, all damp eyes and helpless curiosity.

'He's all yours.' Sophie was extracting several items from her beautiful beaded bag. 'The card that opens the city apartment, the keys for the main house on the

Winterwood estate and the keys for the Porsche. He told me to keep it . . . but I don't think I earned that size of pay-off.'

'I don't want them!' Bella exclaimed in horror as the items were thrust into her hand.

'You're planning to marry Biff or whatever his name is?'

'Well, no, but—'

'Save Rico the trouble of getting extras cut,' Sophie said very drily.

'You've got it all wrong—'

'Good luck. You'll need it. He's anti-love, anti-commitment and anti-marriage. Sensational divorces leave scars,' she murmured tightly, turning to the door. 'It's just a pity that Rico doesn't appreciate that he's not the only one ever to have been hurt!'

Bella was left holding the keys. Sophie had shattered her. She was one very strong lady . . . one very generous lady. After all, had it once occurred to Bella whilst in that container that she was playing around with another woman's man? *Not once.* Maybe she hadn't wanted to recall seeing Rico with Sophie that very first night, emerging from that hotel, climbing into the Bugatti. Suddenly Bella, who prided herself on her principles, saw that she had sacrificed more than one with Rico, and whether it was fair or otherwise she hated him for reducing her to that level.

Head high, she walked back to the table, as beautiful and as remote as a moving statue. Without looking once at Rico, she dropped the keys and the card in front of him. 'I want to go home, Griff.'

'*Hasta la vista, gatita,*' Rico drawled smoothly.

CHAPTER SEVEN

IT HAD taken quite some time for Griff to unload her paintings and possessions from the BMW. He was in an astonishingly good mood. Rico had known the way to Griff's heart. He had promised to recommend him to one of his friends, who was currently enduring the horrors of a broken marriage.

'And once I get *those* kinds of people coming to me for advice,' Griff bored on, 'I'll be offered a senior partnership.'

'Marvellous.' Had he always been this boring, this predictable? She felt awful even thinking that, but couldn't wait to escape.

'It could bring our wedding forward by a year or two—'

'Say that again?' she practically whispered.

Griff gravely outlined his agenda for their future—a three-year engagement, her discovery as an artist to facilitate the expense, marriage only when they had left no stone of possible incompatibility unturned and explored. It was so very sensible that she wanted to tear her hair out, for this was a man whom a few short weeks ago she had believed she would marry, should he ask.

Without warning she belatedly recalled the photographer who had shouted his thanks to Griff before he'd taken off. 'Why did that man with the camera thank you?'

Griff frowned. 'I told him we would be there.'

'You did *what*? Were you also aware that Rico would be there?'

113

'It's his favourite watering-hole, I understand, and I was delighted when he showed up and joined us. It was unfortunate that his date chose to take off early, but there'll be no more undesirable publicity once our engagement is announced in print, complete with photo,' Griff pointed out with pride, blind to the gathering rage and disbelief in Bella's face, he was so patently pleased with himself.

'But I didn't say *yes!*' she hissed.

He took a step back, flinching from her venom.

'The answer is no. I don't want to marry you. Not only are you unfaithful, you are stingy. You pocketed the ring again... You just couldn't bring yourself to part with it!' she reminded him witheringly.

'How dare you call me stingy?'

'And you can take that announcement right back out of the paper again, because I'd sooner starve than be married to a stingy, manipulative man who is more concerned with his image at the office than with me!' Thrusting him bodily out of the dingy hall, Bella slammed the door on him before he had the chance to snap his dropped jaw closed again.

She perched on the step one up from the bottom of the stairs. She was waiting for Rico. He would come. She knew it in her bones. And she was all shaken up just thinking about it. A man who bought women the same way he bought his shirts. Sophie had ripped the scales from her stupid eyes. Anti-love, anti-commitment and anti-marriage. How could she have fallen in love with a man like that?

For it was love. She could no longer lie to herself. Seeing Rico again tonight had torn her apart but it had also made her face the truth. She had fallen violently in love with a man who bonded with women on an immoral basis of keys and gifts of expensive cars, a male who might have remarkable staying power in bed—her cheeks burned—but whose staying power in relationships was abysmal. *Two* months? Even Bella allowed men to last longer than two months...most of the time, she adjusted. Griff had lasted three, but then he worked a lot of overtime, she conceded absently.

And what about the sensational divorce? She should have asked Liz about Rico's failed marriage. It was strange that there had been no mention of it in the papers. Liz was a walking encyclopaedia on celebrity lives and scandals. But then maybe Liz hadn't known, or maybe Liz had just been too good a friend to mention Rico when Bella had gone to such ridiculous lengths to avoid referring to him herself. Poor Liz. She must have used superglue to keep her lips sealed on all the questions she'd been dying to ask!

The mechanical Edwardian doorbell shrilled and made her jump. She unlocked the door.

'You should have a chain on,' Rico grated, striding in. 'Why is this place in total darkness?'

'Hector doesn't like electricity bills!'

Thrusting arrogantly past her, Rico skimmed a hand along the wall, and abruptly the great chandelier above blazed into light. Bella had never seen it illuminated before and she stared up, wondering how it would look without the cobwebs. There was a strangled moan from the landing above.

'Switch that off!' Hector urged in horror. 'Are you trying to ruin me? Have you any idea how many watts that burns?'

'Switch it off, for heaven's sake...before he has a heart attack!'

Rico stared up at the thin figure wrapped in the ragged wool robe and mounted the stairs. 'Mr Barsay...I am Rico da Silva.' He extended a lean hand with awesome cool.

Hector pressed his hand to his palpitating chest instead. 'Switch off that light!' he pleaded.

'I'll pay for it,' Rico drawled smoothly, tugging out his wallet and extracting a crisp note. 'I'm reduced to a shuddering wreck by darkness after my experience in that container. My nerves couldn't stand the strain.'

'Bella has candles—'

'Not enough.' Rico pressed the note apologetically into Hector's trembling hand. 'And I do understand what a struggle it is for you to survive in this house.'

There was no subject dearer to Hector's heart. He managed a brave smile while surreptitiously pocketing the money. '*Hector*!' Bella moaned in embarrassment.

'Women don't understand these things,' Rico sighed.

'I don't like visitors,' Hector snorted. 'But you can stay.' And off he went.

Bella raced upstairs.

'Where do you hang out?' Rico enquired, shooting an incredulous glance over the peeling walls and general air of decay surrounding him. 'In the attic with the bats? No wonder you're off the wall, *gatita*. He's as nutty as a fruitcake.'

'How dare you?' she said, her teeth gritted. 'He can't help being poor—'

'*Poor*?' Rico burst out laughing. 'He could buy and sell everyone else in this street! He has a solid-gold investment portfolio that keeps on raking in the cash year after year.'

'I don't believe you—'

'He has just about everyone fooled but I checked him out. Hector Barsay is stinking rich and he never parts with a penny if he can help it. Charities know not to knock on this door.'

'You've mixed him up with someone else . . . you must have done!'

'Where's your lair?'

Stiff-backed, she mounted the second flight of stairs ahead of him and reluctantly pushed open the door. He reached for the light switch.

'There's no bulb,' she said with pleasure, and then abruptly she recalled her paintings and spun round. 'We'll go downstairs.'

'I wouldn't dream of it. I've always wanted to see a starving artist's garret. Where's the flea-ridden straw pallet and the mousetraps?' he enquired, lifting the solid-silver candelabra by her bed and using the matches sitting beside it. '*Madre de Dios...*' he breathed, surveying the bare room with an emotion akin to incredulous fascination. 'You will think you have entered paradise when I take you home with me!'

'You're not taking me anywhere, Rico.' She folded her arms. In the flickering light from the candles he was a dark silhouette in bronze and black—lithe and sleek and as graceful as a jungle cat. Her mouth went dry.

'Even if you can't paint anything other than blobs in primary colours I'll be your patron,' Rico said smoothly. 'And you deserve that I say that to you. I've learnt more about you in the papers than you ever deigned to tell me.'

She flushed. 'And that should tell you something—'

'That you like to dramatise...that you like to play games?' He shot the demand at her in fast, fluent French. 'You may not attach too much importance to spelling but you speak French, German, Italian and Russian like a native, I believe.'

She tensed even more, her mouth tightening. 'You shouldn't believe everything you read—'

'Do you or don't you?' he raked at her in German.

'OK...OK...guilty as charged!'

'You described yourself to me as a waitress—'

'I'm not ashamed of being a waitress—'

'But you could have been a rocket scientist if you'd wanted to be! Your teachers said you were brilliant—'

'A slight exaggeration—'

'But bone-idle academically and fixated on art...and I have this awful suspicion that you can't paint for peanuts,' Rico bit out harshly. 'Hector's the father you never had and you would very much like to walk in your lousy father's footsteps!'

Bella had turned white. She hadn't expected such a forceful attack as this. Rico was so angry. Why? Did he think that she had made a fool of him? Was she supposed to have reeled off a boastful list of her abilities for his benefit? 'Clever clogs', the other kids had whispered nastily behind her back when she had been at school. Bella had learnt the hard way that it was easier to be average than gifted.

'Biff thinks you're as thick as the proverbial plank; can't understand why the papers are making up so many ridiculous lies,' Rico derided.

'His name is Griff and he does not think I'm thick—'

'"Exquisite on the eye, dizzy as a dodo," he told me cheerfully. He would run a mile if he knew that you were capable of out-thinking, out-guessing and out-plotting his every move!'

Bella compressed her lips. 'What are you doing here?'

'You were waiting for me,' he reminded her smoothly, surveying her with smouldering golden eyes that burned wherever they touched. 'When I saw you in that restaurant I wanted to put my hands round your throat and squeeze hard. Where the hell have you been for the past three weeks? Why the hell did Chief Superintendent Nazenby treat me like a convicted criminal who was dangerous to women and refuse to divulge your whereabouts?'

Bella went pink and managed a jerky shrug. 'It didn't occur to me that you'd ask.'

'This is not Biff you are talking to... this is *Rico*,' he growled, moving forward, his handsome face as hard as iron. 'And I can scent female deviousness a mile away. I offended your pride at the police station, and you removed yourself from my radius to let me learn to appreciate you in your absence. Then magically you reappeared in my favourite restaurant with another man—a man all primed and ready to propose holy matrimony with *me* as an audience!'

'You conceited jerk!' Bella slung at him in disbelief. 'You actually think I would sink to that level to try and trap you?'

'*Si*...' He threw her a seething look of condemnation. 'I might respect you more if you simply admitted how calculating you are!'

'How did you get through the front door with an ego that size?'

'My apologies if I did not rise to your expectation of me throwing a jealous scene! I am not the jealous type.'

'I'll believe you...thousands wouldn't,' she responded sweetly, recognising with a kind of savage pleasure that he had indeed been jealous, and ready to thank him even more sweetly for bringing it to her notice. 'You were rude to me, rude to poor Sophie, and rude to Griff, although it probably went over his head. I don't know what I did to earn that... And as for Sophie, my heart went out to her—'

'What heart?' Rico slashed back viciously. '*Por Dios*...to see you sitting there holding hands with *him*! You got exactly the reaction you expected—'

'I didn't know you would be there!' But she knew that she was talking to a brick wall. Rico was convinced that she had set him up. Griff had set them both up, but Rico would not believe that. Why? Because Griff had been so polite that Rico had written him off as a lame brain. But Griff would never have risked offending someone as powerful and rich as Rico da Silva.

'I want to see these famous paintings, not one of which has ever been sold,' Rico derided, heading for the pile of canvases stacked along the entire length of the spacious room, 'but which Nazenby considers works of

pure genius... *Infierno*! He probably couldn't tell an
old master from a Picasso!'

'No!' Bella planted herself squarely in his path.

'And what happened to your terror of the police force?
I did everything within my power to support you at that
police station,' Rico reminded her rawly, setting her out
of his path with one imperious hand. 'And now Nazenby
talks about you as though you're part of his family!'

'Face that container and you can face anything. I'd
kept up the fear out of habit... *No*, Rico!'

'I want to see them. You live with Hector Barsay and,
unless old age has mellowed him, you have to be accustomed to criticism.'

'Why is it so important for you to see them?' she
wailed in distress.

'Why is it so important for you to prevent me?'

'They're private,' she muttered tightly.

'An artist whose every work is private—how thought-
provoking,' he drawled nastily, flipping back the first
canvas.

'Hector says I'm not ready to be shown yet. He thinks
my interpretation needs a lot more work... more ma-
turity,' she proffered unsteadily, voicing her supposed
flaws in advance.

The silence went on and on. She clutched her hands
together, as nervous as someone watching her children
jay-walking across an accident black spot. Rico shone
the candelabra on about half a dozen, slowly moving
from one to the next. Nothing could be read from the
taut lines of his dark features. Expelling his breath, he
straightened, but he was still studying an oil of children
playing in the mud round a lorry.

'You paint your childhood,' he breathed tautly.

'Not all the time.'

'Hector is not only a miser, he's a liar. He wants to
hold onto you, *es verdad*? His own discovery. He can't
let you go. He hid away from that world out there years

ago, and if he encourages you to exhibit he knows he'll lose you!' Rico sent her a shimmering glance, his expressive mouth compressed into a strangely bloodless line. 'You have extraordinary talent and you cannot possibly require someone like me to tell you that.'

'You like them?'

He set the candelabra back by the bed and stood there, watching her with hooded dark eyes. 'I'm in shock and you know it. Why are you working as a waitress?'

'It pays the rent. I paint in daylight, work at night. I get fabulous tips—'

'I can imagine.'

'The hours suit me.'

'Biff told me you were a catering supervisor, not a waitress—'

Spontaneously, Bella laughed. 'He would say that!'

'With me you'll be what you are—an artist—'

Bella stilled. 'I won't be with you, Rico. Never again,' she swore shakily.

'No more games, *gatita mia*.' He strolled fluidly across the bare boards. Even the way he moved, the effortless grace of that lithe, powerful body, shook her to her very depths. He took out his wallet and extracted a cheque.

'Where did you get this money?'

When Liz had collected her clothes she had also collected the one valuable possession Bella had—a small oil of her mother, painted by her father. Liz had taken it to a top art gallery and sold it for her. She would have made more at auction but she had been desperate to dissolve what she'd seen as her last tie to Rico and settle the debt. The canvas had fetched enough to cover the repairs to the Bugatti and the Skoda.

'That's my business.'

'What did you do?' he asked, indulgently amused. 'Tell Hector you were about to be dragged off to prison?'

'It was my debt. *I* paid it without anyone else's assistance,' she stressed proudly.

'I don't want it. In fact, I refuse to accept it.' Rico tore the cheque in two and let the pieces fall like a statement of intent between them.

'I'll just have to get another one...' In bewilderment she stared at him. 'That was your money—'

'Lovers don't have debts between them,' he purred lazily. 'And if you hadn't smashed up the Bugatti I would never have met you. In retrospect it seems a very small price to pay for the amount of pleasure you've given me.'

Feeling the atmosphere thicken, Bella took a jerky step in retreat. 'Less than a month ago you were going to take me to the police—'

'No... I changed my mind in the lift on the way down to the car park... I was taking you home instead,' Rico drawled with rueful amusement.

'I wouldn't have gone! And would you really have done that to Sophie?'

A winged brow elevated. 'What would it have had to do with her?'

Bella threw him a look of distaste. 'She was living with you at the time... or did you think I hadn't worked that out yet?'

'Sophie had keys for convenience. She never lived with me. I haven't shared a roof with a woman in the past decade. Live-in relationships can get very messy and possessive—'

'And with a two-month limit on your interest it really wouldn't be worth the effort?'

'You're talking to *me* about track records?' Rico threw back his dark head and laughed with a forbidding lack of humour. 'What about yours?'

'*Mine*?'

'You are one flighty lady if one half of what I read is true, *gatita mia.*'

'I am not flighty—'

'No... I'll clip your wings, chain you to the bed when I'm out, take you with me when I go abroad, employ only ugly old men.' He watched her with mesmeric intensity and then he smiled—a brilliant smile of unconcealed triumph. 'Then again, I'm really not that worried. Out of all those men I was the only one you slept with, *es verdad*?'

Outraged by the blazing confidence with which he surveyed her, she said, 'That wasn't how you felt at the time.'

'I'd never made love to a virgin before. You took me by storm.' Rico spread his smooth brown hands with expressive amusement. 'I had to escape to fully appreciate what an enormous compliment it was to be selected out of a cast of thousands to make the grade.'

'I think it's time you left.'

'Only if you come home with me. Don't bother packing. I'll send someone over to clear this place tomorrow.'

Her nails cut purple crescents into her palms. 'Are you asking me to live with you?' she whispered tightly.

He winced. 'Do you have to be so precise? I suggest we spend a month together and take it from there.'

'You said live-in relationships get messy and possessive,' Bella reminded him doggedly.

'That is a risk I'm prepared to take—'

'Briefly,' she inserted, thinking of the month he had designated. Not much of a risk at all.

'—to have you in my bed again,' he completed shortly.

'And that is all you want?'

A spasm of raw impatience flashed across his set features. 'The generation gap, *es verdad*? Have you ever heard of subtlety? *Infierno* ... what the hell am I doing here?'

'When you only came to insult me? I'm wondering too.'

He glowered at her in disbelief. 'How have I insulted you?'

Bella was starting to shake with rage and reaction, much of which, she acknowledged, stemmed from bitter disappointment. 'You offer me a month's trial in your bed as if you're some sultan talking to a little harem slave and you don't think that's an insult?' she spat with unashamed contempt.

Rico merely shrugged and looked levelly back at her. 'What have you got to lose—Biff and the ring he put back in his pocket?' he mocked.

'Maybe...'

'I won't ever offer you a ring, *gatita mia*. If that is your goal, settle for your tame little solicitor and suburbia,' he advised, his lip curling.

Inside herself she ached. Had she had the faintest suspicion that Rico cared for her, she might have settled for the month's trial in the hope that it might develop into something more. That awareness shamed her. How many rules did you break before you began to hate yourself? Every rule she broke as far as Rico was concerned shaved away her self-respect, and without her pride she would be weak. She was an all-or-nothing person.

'Since you've been so frank, I'll match you.' She walked away, working up the courage to do so, her beautiful face deeply troubled, tiny little shivers of high-wire tension rippling through her. 'I grew up with instability, with my mother's love affairs, her broken hearts, her depressions, her humiliations. I will not live like that. I saw how you treated Sophie tonight—'

'Sophie and I were not lovers.'

Bella stared at him in shock.

'Sophie acted as my hostess. We probably would have become intimate,' he admitted, 'but then you and I were kidnapped and everything changed.'

'Everything changed'. Yes, everything had changed for Bella too. Within the space of less than thirty-six hours the entire course of her life had been altered. Bonds had been formed, emotions unleashed and her every desperate attempt to put the clock back had failed.

'It was over before it ever began between Sophie and me. This evening she invited herself,' Rico revealed grimly.

'Even so, you didn't give a damn about her!' Bella accused, recalling his complete detachment from the other woman, knowing that there would be a day when she would earn a similar lack of interest. 'I'm worth more than that.'

'You should have kept that in mind, *querida*...before you offered yourself to me. That was your value, not mine.'

Bella flinched as though she had been struck. She was in love with a total, irredeemable swine. Cleo's bad taste paled beside this demonstration of raw masculine arrogance. She refused to lower herself to the same level.

She thrust her head high. 'I won't do it. I need more.'

'You want marriage.' Rico dealt her a look of supreme derision, but at the back of that derision lurked a simmering pool of explosive rage. 'I said I wanted you. I didn't say I was down on my knees and certifiably insane!'

'I didn't say I wanted marriage!' she gasped strickenly.

'You don't need to. You could spell it out in fireworks above my bank and it would be less obvious than what I see in your face!' he bit out with sudden viciousness as he strode forward and closed hard hands round her forearms before she could retreat. 'I was right all along. You had your price all right. But it's not a price I would even contemplate, and you have to be bloody naïve to imagine that I would be that desperate!'

'I never mentioned marriage!'

'In the next breath you were about to mention children, no doubt,' he scorned. '*Madre de Dios...*'

'I *love* them!' Bella flung at him, losing her head. 'I also want a large fluffy dog and a cat and a pony for them. So take yourself off, Rico! Go find a bimbo to audition for the honour of sharing your precious bed! And if she amuses herself on the side with your gardener or one of your security men you will only be getting what you deserve!'

'*Por Dios...*you may have an IQ higher than my credit rating but you are unhinged.' Rico swore furiously. 'No normal woman would speak like this to me!'

'I'm ashamed I ever let you touch me. I'll be scrubbing myself clean for a month!' she shouted back. 'How dare you come here into my home and talk to me as if I'm some sort of glorified whore? Was I going to get a Porsche as well?'

'Driving lessons,' he raked down at her, his dark head lowering. 'Putting you behind the wheel of a Porsche would be like putting an arsonist in a barn!'

'Don't you dare!' she warned, shaking like a leaf as the scent of him washed over her, as the taut, muscular angles of his hard body met in direct collision with hers.

'You're gasping for it too.'

He kissed her and the world fell away and everything else soared to an ungovernable height of excitement. He closed his arms around her so tightly that she couldn't breathe, but she didn't want to breathe. Dizzy and disorientated, she clung to him, lost in the devastating plunge into passion, her heart racing, her pulses throbbing, every muscle taut with a hunger that dominated and controlled. Heat surged into her loins, making her thighs tremble against the aroused thrust of his manhood. He swept her up in his arms and then dropped her on the ancient feather mattress from a height.

'You're a pushover, *querida*.' He stared down at her, his hard-boned features grim and derisive. 'And you will crawl for that month's trial before I am finished with you!' he stated chillingly.

'Push off, you bastard!' Bella shrieked, her voice cracking.

'And you will stop using language like that,' he hissed in outrage. 'If you want me to treat you like a lady, talk like one!'

'You wouldn't recognise a lady if you fell over one!' she sobbed, out of control with rage and self-loathing. 'I hate you, Rico!'

The door closed. She thumped the pillow with clenched fists. She hadn't buckled. She had been tempted but she hadn't buckled, hadn't surrendered. Why then didn't she feel better? Why had the sound of that door closing filled her with dread? But she knew why, didn't she? He had left her alone again and, for a charged instant, she didn't believe that she could bear the emptiness that stretched ahead without him.

CHAPTER EIGHT

'"A COMPLETE gentleman",' the journalist repeated woodenly, disappointment emanating from her in waves. It might have been an exclusive interview but the content was not of the salacious variety guaranteed to titillate.

'Absolutely,' Bella stressed.

The woman coughed. 'I understand there was only one bed—'

'Mr da Silva slept on the floor.'

'*Mr*? You mean you didn't even get on first-name terms?'

'I *think* of him as Mr da Silva,' Bella muttered.

The brunette sighed. 'He's so gorgeous... He looks so... sexy.'

'Looks can be deceptive.'

'He sounds about as exciting as cold porridge.'

'He did take his jacket off and give it to me to keep me warm when we were escaping!' Bella rushed to assert, fearful that she had overdone her efforts to silence press speculation.

Hector was sitting in the kitchen over a cup of tea.

'The paparazzi will vanish tomorrow when that interview is published,' Bella told him with forced cheer. 'The phone will stop ringing and the doorstep will be clear again. Our lives will return to normal.'

'You should never talk to journalists. They twist things,' he warned her.

Bella cleared her throat and surveyed him reflectively. 'Rico said you were stinking rich...'

Hector choked on his tea. She had to bang him on the back. It was five minutes before he stopped spluttering.

'Absolute rubbish!' he swore weakly.

'But maybe you have a few savings . . . just for a rainy day?'

He looked distinctly cornered and shifty. 'It's possible.'

'And maybe you could afford to put on a few lights now and then. If you have a fall in the dark at your age,' Bella pointed out gently, 'it could be serious. Gramps was never the same after *his* tumble down the stairs. The shock took an awful lot out of him. And then there's the candles, Hector. They're a fire hazard.'

'I'll think it over,' he muttered, looking grey at the grim pictures she had painted. 'You're not thinking of moving out, are you?'

'Where on earth would I go?' she laughed, seeing his fear.

Hector sighed. 'I meant to say to you last night but I fell asleep . . . I used to know da Silva's father, João. He had a tremendous art collection. Old money, of course. Shame the son made such an idiot of himself, but then young people do . . .'

Bella frowned at him and then sat down opposite. 'You're talking about Rico?'

'I was living in Spain then. Must be easily ten years ago,' he mused. 'His divorce case was plastered all over the newspapers out there. He had married some totally unsuitable female. She was an actress or some such thing. She had a string of lovers. There was a young child in-volved as well—'

'A child?' she broke in helplessly.

'It wasn't his child. I remember feeling very sorry for the family, and particularly for the boy, having all that dirty washing dragged out. Ghastly.' Hector shook his head expressively, shooting her a troubled glance. 'Not an experience I should think he came through unscathed. These days he seems to have more of a reputation as a womaniser.'

Bella was shaken by what Hector had told her. A failed marriage she was already aware of but *this* was something else entirely. 'The Press went over my life with a fine-tooth comb... how come they didn't pick up on his marriage?'

'It happened in a different country. He's just been lucky.'

She lay in bed that night mulling the bare facts over. By the sound of it Rico had been badly burnt. And at what age—twenty-one? He couldn't have been much older. The same age as she was now. But Rico might well have been far more vulnerable. Growing up in a rich, privileged and happy family did not necessarily prepare you very well for the darker side of life and the people who used and abused you. In fact money had probably made him more of a target.

He had told her so much but she just hadn't been listening carefully enough. That very first day, when he had quite unreasonably accused her of flaunting herself and trading on her looks, he had also called his attraction to her 'a sick craving'. Right from the outset Rico had fought to deny that attraction. Heavens, did she remind him of his ex-wife? She recalled his preoccupation with the possibility of consequences... 'The honey trap and then the price'... Had it been a shotgun wedding?

Whatever the circumstances, Rico had been betrayed and humiliated, and just thinking about that made Bella's heart go out to him. She was a soft touch. She couldn't help it. Her fury with him from the night before evaporated. For all she knew the suggestion that she *live* with him for a month—an invitation that he had denied ever offering to any other woman—had been a courageous stab at what had felt like a mega-commitment on his part.

On the other hand, it could equally well have been a deeply basic indication of how highly he valued the sexual passion they had shared. Beneath those beautifully tailored suits lurked one very passionate male, no matter how hard he tried to hide it. And he did have a sense of humour. Anyone who could handle Hector without batting an eyelash deserved applause.

He wasn't remotely intimidated by her intelligence either and even in a rage he had been capable of eating his own words and admiring her paintings. He even fitted Gramps' yardstick of eligibility—good education, stable family background, steady employment. And she loved him. It was a shame that he had gone ballistic when she'd mentioned the large fluffy dog, the cat and the pony. Rico did not want children. Still, you couldn't have everything.

And right at this moment you have *nothing*, she reminded herself in exasperation.

Griff rang her mid-morning the next day. 'Bella . . . it would have been kinder to hit the guy with the bottle in the restaurant!'

'What are you talking about?'

'Your exclusive interview . . . priceless, absolutely priceless. Let's do lunch tomorrow. You really should be wearing my ring. It was too late to stop the announcement and I know you didn't mean what you said,' he asserted.

Bella dropped the phone as though she had been burnt. Half an hour later she was standing in a newsagent's, learning that Hector had spoken truly when he'd said that you shouldn't talk to journalists. Rico had been labelled as a boring stuffed shirt, a male so inflated with his own importance that he hadn't even allowed her to call him by his Christian name, the implication being that he was a raging snob. There wasn't even a mention of his taking his jacket off... probably because it might have made him sound human.

Bella cringed, cursing her own stupidity. She checked her watch. She had agreed to work a rare lunchtime shift at the restaurant. In her break she would get on the phone and apologise to him. It had never crossed her mind that anyone could turn their ordeal into sheer comedy, or that so unjust a picture might be drawn. If she had been able to choose a fellow victim out of a million names, she would have chosen Rico every time... She could have wept.

Gaston's was choked to the gills with customers. Serious foodies ate there, studying the yard-long menu with blissful intensity. Bella was loaded with empty plates when she noticed a curious lull in the level of quiet conversation. She turned her head, saw Rico and simply froze.

'What were you paid for that character assassination?' he blazed at her down the length of the entire dining room.

Her staggered gaze clung to him. The tiger had escaped again. Rico in a rage. He strode across the floor in two long, lithe strides, indifferent to the turning heads, the buzz of conjecture. '*How much?*' he breathed in a tone that quivered with fierce emotion.

There was a look of savage betrayal in his brilliant dark eyes. She couldn't bear it. It cut her to pieces. She forgot she was holding the plates. They dropped with an almighty crash. She barely noticed. 'Nothing...'

'You hate me that much?' he shot at her from between clenched teeth.

'No... no,' she whispered, on the brink of tears, appalled that he had taken it so badly, making the worst possible interpretation of that foolish interview.

'I do not appreciate being lampooned in print. It was a pack of lies!' he condemned with raw distaste.

'All I was trying to do was get rid of the reporters...they were upsetting Hector,' Bella muttered frantically.

'And regrettably we're everywhere you look,' a wry voice added from a nearby table in what just might have been a friendly warning.

Exhaling his breath in a sudden hiss, Rico surveyed her, his dark gaze chillingly cold. In the space of a moment he had switched from seething rage to black ice, his strong face clenched hard, his mouth twisting. 'I had you taped from the beginning. No pay, no play...*es verdad*?' he murmured in a derisive undertone.

She had never played poker but she caught his drift. Her cheeks burned. Her lashes swept up on her anguished eyes. 'It's not like that...'

'It's over,' Rico drawled with lethal finality, and swung away.

Every skin-cell in her body vibrating with raw tension, Bella watched him stride towards the exit. And she knew that if she let him go she would never see him again. Her nervous paralysis gave. Tearing the chintzy apron from round her waist, she flung her hovering boss a look of apology and took off after Rico.

He was already climbing into the limousine waiting by the kerb. As she raced across the pavement he stilled and straightened, one lean hand planted on the door. Glittering dark eyes hit her in near physical assault. 'What now?' he demanded.

'I'll play...I mean—' gritting her teeth, cursing her fair skin as it heated, she sealed her lips again and sucked in oxygen '—I'll move in with you.'

His gaze narrowed, sliced even deeper into hers, tension tautening his set features. 'You surprise me—'

'Well, you'd better not surprise *me*,' she warned fiercely. 'You'd better treat me right!'

Sudden vibrant amusement banished his stasis. He
reached for her in one supple movement and pulled her
to him, his hands splaying across the swell of her hips
as he looked down at her. 'You won't regret it, I promise
you,' he assured her huskily.

'If you don't shift this car you're going to get a ticket,'
she muttered, her heartbeat thundering in her ears as her
gaze collided dizzily with his smouldering golden eyes.

But he lowered his head to hers, one hand skimming
up her back to wind into her tumbling hair. Their lips
met slowly, almost hesitantly, and she trembled, the
amount of emotion she was holding back flooding
through her in powerful waves. With a ragged groan he
forced her closer and took her mouth with a sudden,
explosive hunger that made the ground fall away beneath her feet. Her hands closed round him convul-
sively, holding him to her. And she knew then that when
the time came to walk away it would rip her apart.

The limo got a ticket before it rejoined the slow-moving
traffic. Bella looked at Rico, every pulse still racing, her
heart pounding. It was the first time in her life that she
had made a decision that already felt like a foregone
conclusion.

A part of her feared the devastating strength of what
he could make her feel. Reason hadn't powered her
change of heart. She had reacted on instinct and she was
still in shock because of it. He had walked away from
her. It had cut her in two, forced her into compromise.
But she was painfully aware that she was entering the
relationship with needs and expectations that Rico might
not be able to meet.

'I'm flying to Tokyo in the morning for a three-day
conference. You can come with me,' he murmured
smoothly.

And Rico might also have needs and expectations that
she might not be able to meet, Bella registered abruptly.
She wasn't some little bimbo, ready to drop everything

to become a twenty-four-hour handmaiden, programmed to serve with a smile and satisfy every masculine demand.

'I'll be working—'

'*Por Dios*!' he gritted in disbelief. 'Waiting tables?'

'After the number of plates I broke and my departure
at the busiest hour of the day, you can forget that,' she
said ruefully. 'No. I'll concentrate on my painting for a
while.'

'Then you can come to Tokyo,' he asserted forcefully.

'And what am I going to do with myself all day while
you do whatever you do at the conference?'

'Shop,' he retorted impatiently.

'I am not that heavily into shopping, Rico.'

'Naturally I will be paying the bills.'

'When I said that I would move in with you I somehow
missed out on the fact that you planned to pay me for
my services.' Bella shot him a furious look. 'I am not
going to be a kept woman!'

Rico treated her to a fulminating stare, visibly hanging
onto his temper. 'I was not aware that I used that
designation.'

'You didn't need to,' she said tightly.

'*Basta* . . . so I go alone! Leave it there!' he ground out
with raw bite, patently dissatisfied and antagonised by
her response.

He just doesn't know any better, she told herself painfully. He was accustomed to having his own way with
her sex. Sophie hadn't been offered a Porsche for acting
as his hostess alone. He might not have slept with her
but it had been a pay-off. She hadn't earned it, the blonde
had said bluntly. Bella's nostrils flared with distaste. If
Rico knew what was good for him, he would keep the
financial aspect out of their relationship. Bella might not
be rich but she considered herself his equal on every other
level.

'Where are we going?' she asked abruptly.

'My estate... I'm taking you home with me.' Rico's mouth compressed. 'Don't tell me... you have an objection to that as well?'

'If you want to rescue a stray, try Battersea Dog's Home!'

'What the hell is the matter with you?' he suddenly exploded.

'I just don't like being taken over as if I'm some sort of cypher!' She swallowed hard, feeling the dismaying sting of tears in her eyes. 'Look... this—'

'Maybe now that you appreciate that the dog, the cat and the pony will be neither required nor appropriate you're having second thoughts!' he grated in a tense undertone.

'I seriously doubt that I'll be with you long enough for it to become a pressing problem!' Bella was angered and embarrassed at having her own words thrown back in her face.

He went rigid, his jaw-line squaring. 'Don't miscalculate and make it one.'

Bella paled. 'I wouldn't do something like that!' She was shocked by the suggestion that he thought she might.

Abruptly Rico muttered an imprecation and released his breath. 'How can I even say that to you after the risks we ran a few weeks ago?' he murmured drily. 'Let us face facts; we are fortunate indeed that you are not now pregnant.'

Bella bent her head, suppressing an urge to tell him that she was only now expecting the confirmation that their passion was to have no further consequences. Why worry him unnecessarily? It wasn't as if *she* was worried that that confirmation would not arrive. It was extremely unlikely that conception could have taken place at that time of her cycle, she reminded herself, and it was precisely because of that unlikelihood that she had not allowed herself to spend the past three weeks anxiously fretting.

'Becoming a father is not one of your ambitions, I take it.'

'No, definitely not on my agenda. A complication I will happily do without.' His bronzed face was shuttered, taut. 'How did we get onto this subject?'

'You started it.'

'Come here...' With a slightly twisted smile, he stretched out both hands and drew her closer. 'If this feels like a big step to you, *gatita*, it feels just as big to me,' he confided almost harshly, studying her from beneath thick ebony lashes. 'If I get it wrong sometimes, try to make allowances.'

Her tension evaporated. He hadn't found it easy to make that admission and she loved him all the more for making it. Asking her to live with him had been a very real commitment on his terms, she registered, a relieved feeling of contentment enclosing her, smoothing over the ragged edges of her nerves.

'You've been trying to take me home with you ever since you met me,' she whispered.

'With a notable lack of success,' Rico murmured thickly, tugging her relentlessly across the space that still separated them, dark eyes firing gold.

'But you're very persistent.'

'And if I say please...?'

'The world's your oyster,' Bella affirmed, barely able to think straight that close to him.

He linked his arms around her but he tilted his head back, narrowly appraising her. 'You have stars in your eyes, *gatita*. That worries me.'

'You have a fear of being trapped. That worries me even more.'

'Why did you talk to the Press?' he enquired flatly, ignoring her sally.

'I told you why. I just wanted to bring it all to an end. And I thought that if I made it clear that nothing happened between us they would leave me alone—'

'So you lied.'

'I could hardly tell the truth!' But she flushed, her eyes troubled, her mouth faintly mutinous. 'OK...I lied.'

'Don't ever do it again. Don't lie to me and don't lie about me,' Rico told her with level emphasis. 'In fact don't talk about me at all. What is between us is private.'

'I know that!'

'This one time I give you the benefit of the doubt and I forgive you.'

'What's that supposed to mean?'

He surveyed her with cynical dark eyes. 'Bella ... I'm not a fool. I can add two and two. Less than forty-eight hours ago you handed me a cheque for a considerable sum of money. Today the article appeared. Obviously you were paid for that interview.'

She sprang back from him in consternation. 'That money came from the sale of a painting!'

Rico elevated an ebony brow, clearly unimpressed. 'I don't have you on a pedestal, *gatita*. So you don't need to worry about falling off one. I don't expect perfection but I do expect honesty. Who would pay that much for the work of an unknown artist?'

'It wasn't one of *my* paintings!' she flared back at him, both angered and hurt by his lack of trust in her. She would not even have considered accepting money for talking about him to the Press. 'It was one Ivan did of my mother—'

'*Qué dices*?' Rico interrupted, abruptly jerking up out of his lounging position, his attention fully arrested.

'And, before you ask me why I didn't think of selling it that day I came to the bank to tell you I had no insurance, I'll tell you why,' Bella said tightly. 'I forgot about it. I've had it all my life. It didn't occur to me until a few weeks ago that it was a valuable asset which could be sold.'

His incandescent golden eyes bored into her. 'You sold a painting of your mother by your father... to pay me back? Are you crazy?' he launched at her.

Bella blinked at him in bewilderment. 'What else could I do?'

'Where was it sold?' he demanded.

'What does that matter?'

'*Where*?'

She told him.

'If it's already been sold, you'll only have yourself to thank!' he shot at her furiously after he had instructed his chauffeur to head for the art gallery. '*Por Dios*...you don't need to take lessons on how to make me feel bad!'

'I owed you money. It had to be repaid somehow.'

'We were lovers! What do you think I am?' he blazed back at her. 'A debt collector?'

'You are in banking,' she retorted helplessly, infuriated by the reaction she was receiving. Selling that painting had been a considerable sacrifice and she resented the assurance that it had been an unnecessary one. 'And if you think that I was content to believe that just because we had briefly shared a bed I no longer needed to worry about the fact that I owed you thousands of pounds you don't know me at all! I also had to cover the repairs to Hector's Skoda—'

Rico said something incredibly rude about the Skoda.

'We don't all slink about in status-symbol cars!' Bella hissed. 'Why did you tell your driver to go to the art gallery?'

'If the painting's still there, naturally I will buy it back for you.'

'You buy that painting, it's *yours*,' Bella warned him fiercely.

She sat in the car fuming while he was in the art gallery, having flatly refused to accompany him. If he hadn't been so damned suspicious and cynical, he would never have known where she'd got the money from! A debt was a debt. She didn't want it written off. Maybe the money didn't mean much to Rico but it was the principle that mattered.

He swung back into the car and he wasn't empty-handed. He settled the small canvas on her lap. 'Here . . . take Mummy back,' he said very drily.

Bella squinted down at Cleo's familiar features. Her throat ached but she was stubborn. 'I told you I wouldn't accept it.'

'*Madre de Dios* . . .' Rico bit out with raw impatience. 'I could shake you until your teeth rattle!'

'What did you pay for it?'

Grudgingly he told her.

'They saw you coming. You were ripped off. It isn't one of Ivan's best.'

Rico stabbed a button and the window beside him purred down. 'I'll just chuck it out, then, shall I?'

A lean hand closed with purpose round the frame. Involuntarily Bella's gaze clashed with smouldering golden eyes and she gaped. 'You'd do it, wouldn't you?' Her fingers curved protectively round the disputed article.

'You drive me crazy sometimes.' He slung her a fulminating glance and buzzed up the window again.

And sometimes he shook her rigid. He *would* have thrown it out. He had called her bluff and Bella was not accustomed to having her bluff called. She had finally met her match in temper and tenacity. For the first time she was in a relationship where she was not the dominating partner.

'Are you planning to pay me rent?' Rico enquired smoothly.

'Don't be ridiculous!'

'But I sense that money promises to be a bone of contention. If we were married would you feel like this?'

'Of course not,' she said, and then wished she hadn't.

'Illuminating... Clearly I have to suffer for not offering that band of gold,' he murmured sardonically.

She ignored the crack about the wedding ring, barely trusting herself to speak.

'Shut up, Rico...'

'Maybe I should,' he conceded silkily. 'Maybe this is one of those times when you need to make allowances for me.'

Bella was seething. She gritted her teeth.

'This promises to be a deeply challenging relationship. I'm used to having my own way,' he volunteered unapologetically.

'Tell me something I don't know.'

Silence fell. She got lost in her own thoughts. She studied Cleo with far less judgemental eyes than usual. 'I go with my feelings,' her mother had said. And that was exactly what Bella was doing with Rico, had done with Rico even in that wretched container when they'd first made love. No wonder that emotion-driven surrender had filled her with turmoil. Bella always liked to know where she was going. She liked important things cut and dried. But now she had a future in front of her that was a giant unknown.

She surfaced from her introspection as the limousine purred through tall, electronic gates and up a long, winding drive—the Winterwood estate, she gathered, scanning the great sweep of landscaped parkland with curious eyes. In the early summer sunlight of late afternoon the setting was idyllic.

'Do you like the country?'

Bella shrugged a narrow shoulder, struggling not to gape as a vast ancestral pile in stone swam into view round the next bend. It was a magnificent house, designed with all the grace and understated elegance of the eighteenth century. The limousine swept up onto the gravelled frontage and even the soft crunch of the wheels somehow sounded filthy rich. She moistened suddenly

dry lips, quite overpowered. What the heck was she doing
here with him?

She was wearing a denim skirt with a carefully frayed
hem and a T-shirt. She had no make-up on. Her hair
was all mussed—*his* fault. And there he was, im-
maculate as usual, all sleek and sophisticated in a pearl-
grey suit that fitted like a glove and screamed expensive
tailoring. They were the original odd couple. If she lost
him at a party, she would be thrown out as a gatecrasher.

The chauffeur opened the door. Bella stepped out,
feeling more and more as though she had stepped into
Brideshead Revisited. And then she saw the rosebeds and
grimaced.

'What's wrong?' He sounded incredibly anxious, as
if he was primed to her every move and change of
expression.

'Rico, roses are supposed to riot, not march in lines
like soldiers. That looks like council planting at its worst.'
Then she flushed. 'Sorry, that wasn't very polite of me.'

He smiled at her. 'I don't expect you to be polite—'

'Thanks for the vote of confidence.'

'What I meant was...' he placed an arm around her
narrow back '...you just say what you think. It's a very
unusual trait in the world I move in—'

'Sure, you know loads of dreadful people who have
tact and good manners!'

'I like your honesty. It disconcerts me from time to
time,' he murmured, 'but I find it very attractive.'

'Why are you being so *nice* all of a sudden?' she asked
suspiciously.

'This is going to be your home. I want you to relax
here, not behave like a guest,' he asserted.

'I thought I was only here to visit for a month.'

'*Bella*!' he grated.

'Sorry, was I being disconcerting?' She chewed at her
lower lip. 'But you know you have to be up front about

things like that. At the end of the month we put our cards on the table and if it's not working out—'

'We try harder,' he slotted in fiercely.

Bella had been about to conclude that she would move out with no hard feelings...at least, none that she would show.

An elderly little man in a dark suit was awaiting them below the imposing pillared entrance. 'Good evening, Mr da Silva...madam.'

Bella very nearly went off into whoops of laughter. Dear God, he had a butler, a real *live* butler! Her mouth wobbled.

'This is Miss Jennings, Haversham.'

'Miss Jennings.'

'H-Haversham,' she acknowledged, her face frozen as she fought back her giggles.

Rico walked her into a huge, echoing, tiled hall. She felt like someone on a National Trust tour—a member of the paying public, programmed to gawp. She trembled and reckoned that she was winning until a voice said from behind them, 'And what time would you like dinner to be served, sir?'

That was it. Bella went off into gales of laughter. 'Sorry!' she gasped, bending over and hugging her aching ribs as amusement bubbled out of her convulsed throat.

'Seven,' Rico told his butler in a strained tone. 'Are you going to share this joke?' he asked as the stately footsteps of Haversham retreated.

'Definitely not. You wouldn't appreciate it.' Wiping her damp eyes, Bella pulled herself together with difficulty.

'Try me.'

'I thought butlers died out around half a century ago.'

'Haversham came with the house,' Rico told her very seriously, as if he was excusing himself for possessing one of a dying breed.

Bella shook her head, vibrant hair flying like flames round her shoulders. 'Rico... this is another world for me.'

'And you don't like what you've seen of it?'

She grinned. 'No, I'm fascinated.'

'Would you like me to show you around?'

Standing there in the stray patch of sunlight arrowing through a tall sash-window, he looked so good that she couldn't take her eyes off him. Six feet four inches of spectacular masculinity. Visually she adored every extravagantly gorgeous inch of him, her heart accelerating like a racing car screeching round a bend at a hundred-plus miles an hour. She felt her breasts stir and swell inside the cups of her bra, helplessly struggled to fight the electric tension that was wantonly taking her over.

'Bella...' he murmured unsteadily, his shimmering golden eyes suddenly hotly pinned to her.

Emboldened by the discovery that he could look helpless too, Bella smiled, all female. 'Turned very coy all of a sudden, haven't you?'

There was nothing coy about the manner in which he grabbed her, and there was nothing cool about the manner in which he kissed her breathless halfway up the fabulous staircase. She wound her arms round his neck and let him carry her. She wasn't sure that her own legs were up to the feat.

He kicked the door shut on a wonderfully elegant bedroom, decorated in eau-de-Nil with accents of pale gold. He brought her down on the canopied bed and she laughed again, a slim hand stretching up to flick playfully at an exquisite hand-made tassel. 'Who did your decorating?'

'My sister, Elena.'

'She has style... but only a sister would have put you in a room this feminine.' She kicked off her shoes.

'You look incredibly beautiful,' he breathed, his gaze roaming intently over her as he came down on the bed beside her.

Bella reached out and caught his silk tie, drawing him down to her, drowning in the slumbrous glow of his eyes. Their mouths connected, clung, and she went weak, letting her head fall back again. He followed her down, prising her lips apart with the tip of his tongue, ravishing the moist interior that she opened to him with a ragged groan.

She pulled his jacket off, tore at his tie, and as he fought his way out of his shirt let her palms smooth up over the warm, hard wall of his muscular chest, her fingertips teasing at the dark whorls of hair in her path. With an earthy growl he brushed her hands away, thrust her T-shirt up and found her breasts.

It was her turn to gasp and quiver as his expert fingers pushed up her bra and tugged at her engorged nipples. Her back arched in a blinding wave of intolerable excitement.

'You have the most exquisite breasts,' he breathed, grazing her swollen lower lip with his teeth. 'So sensitive . . .'

His dark head swooped and seized a rose-pink bud. Her blood pressure rocketed sky-high. She dug her hands into his hair, driven nearly mindless with the hot, drugging pleasure. She went out of control without a murmur, her heart slamming against her ribcage, every nerve-ending raw with sensation.

He ran a hand up the length of one slim thigh, ruthlessly wrenching her skirt out of his path. Their mouths met again in a torturously hungry mating, and she was shaking, trembling, her hips shifting upwards in a primitive rhythm, all consciousness centred and driven by the erotic brush of his fingers skating over the taut triangle of cloth still dividing her from him.

She burned and panted for breath as he tugged the briefs away and discovered the damp, hot secret of her desire. Intolerable excitement held her in its grip. Suddenly he was pushing her back, shifting over her, unexpectedly stilling when she was poised with anticipation on the furthest edge, every nerve ready to scream with frustration.

'Don't stop!' she gasped.

She felt his hands, roughly impatient on her thighs, and then, with a suddenness that stole her breath away, he thrust into her hard and deeply. An ecstatic cry escaped her, wanton in the depth of need it expressed. She stretched up, kissing his throat, licking the salt from his skin, adoring him. But he pushed her back, arching over her like a primitive god, demanding absolute control, thrusting harder and faster, filling her again and again with the driving force of his manhood. The tension exploded inside her and she jerked like a doll under him, her teeth clenching, a wild, excited cry torn from her as the waves of violent pleasure engulfed her.

Lying shattered and winded in the circle of his arms, listening to the ragged edge of his breathing, she was conscious of a surge of love so intense that it hurt. She rubbed her cheek sensuously against his sweat-dampened shoulder.

'*Dios* . . . we didn't even get our clothes off.' Rico stretched luxuriantly against her. 'I planned a romantic dinner, champagne—'

She wrinkled her nose. 'Predictable.'

'Life is not very predictable around you,' he conceded lazily, and withdrew from her.

Belatedly she understood that pause before he'd possessed her. He had been protecting her. Birth control. She brushed a hand abstractedly over her breasts, conscious of a slight ache that was new to her experience. It had translated into an intense sensitivity when he'd touched her . . . She tensed, the sudden memory of a pregnant friend complaining about the soreness of her breasts flying through her head, jolting her. No, next door to impossible, she christened the fear which followed. Any day now she would know that she was all right. With determination she pushed the concern back out of her mind.

Without warning, strong hands settled beneath her as Rico scooped her up into his arms. 'Why so serious?' he murmured curiously.

'Me...*serious*?' Bella forced a laugh, emerald-green eyes fastening on him, cold fear burrowing up momentarily inside her. 'I was miles away.'

'I want you here,' he told her, setting her down in the beautiful *en suite* bathroom and peeling her T-shirt off.

She reddened. 'I can take my own clothes off.'

'I want to take them off.'

'You think I'm a doll or something?'

'It's an excuse to keep my hands on you,' he breathed. 'And right now I would settle for any excuse.'

Her gaze colliding with lustrous dark eyes, she stretched up and linked her hands round his strong brown throat. She felt dizzy with happiness, and generous. 'You don't need an excuse,' she whispered with all the natural warmth that lay at the core of her temperament.

'Tomorrow will come too soon. Tokyo...' Rico murmured. 'I'll send Kenway in my place—just this once.'

And then he covered her mouth with erotic precision, his hands buried in her hair. It was a long time before they made it into the shower.

CHAPTER NINE

'THEY belong to my sister. They should fit.'

Bella surveyed the riding gear with concealed amusement. 'I could wear my jeans.'

'You'll feel more comfortable in these. Jeans can be very constricting,' Rico informed her.

'You're planning for me to look impressive round your stables?' She looked at him with mockery.

'I intend to teach you how to ride.'

Of course, far be it from Rico to ask if she could already ride. He specialised in making assumptions. But then it was encouraging that he should want her to share a pastime which he obviously enjoyed. Obediently sliding into the borrowed outfit, she watched him out of the corner of her eye and wondered where the past two days had gone. Time was already slipping through her fingers like sand.

They hadn't made it down for dinner that first night. They had picnicked like starving adolescents at the kitchen table in the early hours. The next morning she had insisted on going up to London to see Hector and supervise the removal of her possessions. She had wanted to leave her paintings behind but that had provoked an argument, so she had given way. Rico had already had a room cleared for her to use a studio. Filled with natural light, it was an artist's dream, and if there was such a thing as inspiration, she reflected wryly, Winterwood would surely provide it.

Although not according to Hector. Bella's cheeks flushed as she recalled his reaction to her chosen change of abode. He had been shocked, unhappy and dismayed. In all fairness, what other response could she have expected? Hector was of a different generation. But seeing his disappointment in her had upset her.

'If he cared about you he'd want to marry you,' he had told her sternly, and she had bitten her lip and refused to argue. Only time would tell whether Rico cared or not.

'Come closer.' Rico beckoned with an imperious hand. 'Horses sense fear. It makes them nervous.'

'You think I'm afraid?'

'Why else would you be standing so far back?' Arrogantly he took her hand and showed her how to become acquainted with the velvet-nosed bay mare that was shuffling restively on the cobbles while a groom saddled her up. 'Sheba's a little fresh. I'll put you on her in the paddock...on a leading rein.'

'Gosh...it looks a long way up,' Bella twittered, striving to look scared.

'I'll be with you. You'll be fine. *Dios*...I told him I wouldn't be riding,' he bit out impatiently, only then noticing that the other groom had already tacked up the glossy grey stallion on the other side of the yard.

And I told him you would be, she thought. Grasping Sheba's reins, Bella planted a foot in the stirrup and mounted up in one smooth movement.

Halfway across the yard Rico swung back. 'Bella!' he yelled, clearly thinking that she was being recklessly daring to impress.

'Last one over the fence is a wimp!' she called over her shoulder.

Sheba was fresh all right. Given her head, she took off like a bullet out of a gun, racing for the fence. Bella gloried in the wind tearing at her hair and the speed. It was over a year since she had been on a horse. She heard the thunder of pursuit and grinned. Next time Rico would *ask* whether or not she could do something before he *told* her she was going to learn.

Sheba sailed over the fence like a champion and gal-
loped across the rolling parkland. Rico's stallion thundered past and was reined in on a rise beside a clump
of massive oak trees. Sheba was slowing down by then.
Bella let her trot the last hundred yards.

Two long strides carried Rico to her side as she slid
down off the mare's back.

'Sorry...but I couldn't resist it.' Her spontaneous smile
lit up her whole face as she turned to him.

Her smile lurched and died as Rico closed angry hands
round her forearms. 'Don't ever get on one of my horses
again without a hard hat!' he seethed down at her.

'I never wear a hat.'

'You will... If you don't, you don't ride,' he spelt
out flatly, pale beneath his golden skin. 'And only an
idiot would jump a fence like that on a strange mount!'

'Or an idiot who asked the groom first how she per-
formed. He told me she jumped like she was on springs.'
Bella looked up at him, into still grim dark eyes, and
groaned. 'I gave you a fright. I'm sorry.'

'Where did you learn to ride?'

'Well, not in a paddock on a leading rein.' She threw
herself down on the lush grass and turned her face into
the sunlight. 'Cleo had friends we sometimes stayed with.
They had horses. I was crazy about them. And Gramps
kept stables—'

'Stables?'

'Boarding, riding lessons, all that sort of stuff.' She
linked her hands round her raised knees and stared down
the rolling slope into the distance. 'The business went
bust when I was nineteen. He broke a hip while I was
at college. He could've asked me to come home but he
didn't. By the time I realised how bad things were the
bank was calling in his loan. All he needed was a little
more time but they pushed him to the wall.'

'I gather you tried to persuade the bank otherwise.'

'A waste of my breath.' Bella grimaced. 'And when the horses had to be sold Gramps just gave up. He didn't own the stables. He had to move out into a council house in the village. It killed him.'

'Why do you blame yourself?'

Bella tensed, unprepared for someone saying out loud what she had often thought. 'I could've stopped it happening.'

'How?'

'I could've run the place for him until he got back on his feet.'

'But he obviously didn't want you to drop out of college, *gatita*. And what business experience did you have? Why blame yourself when you lost your home as well?'

'Fiddlesticks,' she said, with a wry curve to her expressive mouth. 'A little tub of an elderly Shetland pony called Fiddlesticks. I was more upset about him being sold. Silly really—I mean, he was only a pet. I was far too big to ride him.'

Rico tugged her back against his chest. '*Dios* . . . loath as I am to admit it when you have been showing off, you're a terrific rider.' His breath stirred her hair, the familiar scent of him blissfully enveloping her.

She felt at peace in Rico's arms and that worried her. At peace was the last thing she ought to have felt around him. This was an interlude for him. It wouldn't last. He didn't even want it to last. He wanted a passionate affair and an open door to freedom at the end of it. No strings, no complications, no recriminations. He had made that resoundingly clear.

She felt mean and she acted accordingly. 'Tell me about your ex-wife.'

The strong muscles in his arms drew taut. 'What do you want to know?'

'Her name . . . that would be a start.'

'Margarita.'

'And then maybe you could tell me why you're so bitter,' she dared.

'I am not bitter.'

'Do I remind you of her?'

'Not at all. She was small, black-haired, blue-eyed.'

'Beautiful?'

'Stunning.'

'You could ease up on the superlatives if you like,' she told him. 'So how did you meet?'

'A nightclub. She was an actress but I had no idea how ambitious she was. In fact I never really knew her at all,' he admitted flatly. 'I was twenty, she was two years older. I didn't know the difference between love and sexual obsession. At that age *everything* feels so intense. When she told me she was pregnant I married her.'

'Yes,' she whispered softly.

'Once he was born, Margarita dropped any pretence of wishing to be a mother and went back to the film world,' he said drily. 'I tried very hard to make the marriage work. Everyone had told me I was making a mistake. I was determined to prove them wrong...and I trusted her.

'Even when I found her in bed with another man I didn't realise that he was one of many. She would have slept with anyone capable of furthering her career. She was drunk that night. She told me how many others there had been. The next morning she moved out and moved in with her producer. I instigated the divorce...'

'What else could you have done?' Bella leant her head back against him, understanding all that he had left unsaid. He had been used, kicked in the teeth and dumped. She waited for him to mention the little boy again, realised that he hadn't even referred to him by name, and also that he had not told her that that child had not been his.

'Margarita made it a battle, and she revelled in the publicity until it turned on her,' he drawled. 'Her career nosedived after the divorce. Nobody came out of it happy.'

Had he still been in love with his ex-wife? His grim intonation suggested regret to Bella. Regret for what? She wanted to probe deeper but resisted the temptation. She knew that she would drag it all out of him eventually. But now, she sensed, was not the time.

'But I learnt a lot from Margarita,' Rico murmured with satire.

Nothing good, Bella thought. He didn't trust women. He was always looking for ulterior motives. He didn't believe in permanence. And marriage for him had been a destructive trap from which he had gained nothing. But one truth he had spoken. He had said that he wasn't bitter and on that count she believed him. He had come to terms with that part of his past.

Why, then, did she sense that there was a whole lot missing from what he was telling her? He had glossed over the subject of the child. But then he wasn't that fussed about kids anyway, was he? In a marriage as bad as that, and as short-lived, it might well have been a relief not to be linked to his ex-wife by a tie as unbreakable as that of a child.

'What did you learn?'

He settled back on the lush meadow grass and looked down at her, scanning her vibrant face with glittering dark eyes. 'That I don't have to get married to enjoy myself. That what we have here, now, is far more exciting than being welded together by an empty contract full of promises destined to be broken. If we stay together it will be a free and uncomplicated choice—'

'Nothing's that uncomplicated.'

'Trust me...I trust you,' he breathed, lowering his dark head. 'I know you took a risk on me. I know this wasn't your dream. This has to be the first time in my life that a woman hasn't wanted anything from me but myself.'

'And I'm only after your body, so you can feel safe.'

With an appreciative grin he slid a hard thigh between hers, pinning her in place, studying her slumbrously from beneath the thick veil of his black lashes. 'When you look at me like that you fill me with uncontrollable lust, *gatita mia*.'

'But then that doesn't take much,' she muttered, dizzily drowning in his intent gaze as he shifted fluidly against her, letting her feel the hard thrust of his arousal.

Bella was down at the stableyard one morning when she was told that a visitor was waiting to see her. Returning to the house, she stilled in the doorway of her studio, taut with disbelief at the sight of a complete stranger calmly leafing through her paintings. 'What are you doing?' she demanded sharply. 'Who are you?'

The man straightened, seemingly unaware of his offence, and crossed the room. He extended a polite hand. 'Dai Matheison ... Rico asked me to pay you a visit next time I was in the area.'

Rico had asked him? Bella's face froze. 'The Matheison Gallery, right?' she murmured, mentioning the prestigious gallery with distinct coolness.

'Try not to hold it against me.' Shrewd blue eyes read her taut facial muscles.

'Rico didn't tell me you were coming.' She wanted to leap up and down with sheer rage and embarrassment. How dared Rico humiliate her like this? Unknown artists did not receive personal visits from the owner of the Matheison Gallery.

'Between you, me and the gatepost,' Dai Matheison said drily, 'I didn't want to. But if what I have so far managed to see is a sample of your work Rico did us both a favour. I'm doing an exhibition in late September. I'm willing to include you if you're interested.'

Her teeth gritted. 'Thank you but I don't think—'

'Rico may be a friend, but don't insult me by assuming that I would issue such an invitation on that basis alone,' he cut in smoothly. 'If I didn't think you were worthy of my gallery's reputation, Miss Jennings, God Himself would not persuade me otherwise.'

Bella reddened, sharply disconcerted. 'I—'

He handed her a card. 'Call me if you're interested and don't leave it too late. I need an answer soon.'

'Mr Matheison, I'm sorry—'

'Not half as sorry as I am.' He smiled with rueful amusement. 'I was looking forward to shooting Rico down in flames. But after what I've seen here I shall have to grit my teeth and say, Thank you for the tip. You're even more talented than he said you were.'

He was gone before she could gather her wits again. In one explosive stride she reached the nearest phone and dialled Rico's private number.

'Did you remember to call the caterers?' he asked straight off, reminding her about the party he was planning to hold in a fortnight's time.

'*Yes*. Dai Matheison has just been here!'

There was a moment of silence.

'And?' he responded calmly.

'And nothing, Rico! How dare you do that to me?'

'I have other contacts.'

'Stuff your bloody contacts!' she hissed. 'If you must know, he's willing to show me, but that's not the point—'

'That was exactly the point,' Rico interrupted with unhidden satisfaction.

'You had no right to interfere.'

'You and your giant insecurity complex were likely to avoid the issue into the next century,' he informed her. 'So I took care of it for you.'

His lack of remorse only inflamed her more. In all her life she had rarely felt as mortified as Rico had made her feel. 'You humiliated me,' she condemned shakily.

'And if you can't see that, then there's not a lot of hope for us!'

'Be brief, Bella,' he sighed, refusing to take her seriously. 'I have two diplomats waiting to see me.'

'I make my own breaks. I don't need you to pull the strings for me. Dai Matheison didn't want to come here. He thought he was coming to see your little bimbo's etchings—'

'Now he knows differently,' Rico returned with exasperated unconcern. 'Tell me, is there a point to this howling melodrama? You should be grateful I had that amount of faith in you. I told you I'd be your patron—'

'You just can't accept what I give!' she accused in stark distress. 'You're not happy unless you think you're paying for what I do in bed!'

'Bella, no man in his right mind would pay for this. I'll call you from Edinburgh.' The assurance was icy cold. The phone went dead.

Throwing herself face down on a sofa, she burst into floods of tears, shocking herself. She felt out of control, desperately hurt, desperately confused.

They had been together for three and a half wonderfully happy weeks. But sometimes she got scared; sometimes she admitted to herself that temperamentally she was not cut out for a relationship in which she could not say openly, honestly, I love you. She guarded her tongue more and more. It had become harder to keep up the free-and-easy sallies that demanded nothing, asked for no reassurance, never mentioned the future. And all of a sudden Bella knew that she was facing up to the reality of their relationship.

Rico didn't want any more from her. He wanted her passion, not her love. She felt like somebody squeezed into a box that was becoming suffocating. Holding her emotions back didn't come naturally to her. The longer she held them in, the more dangerous they felt. On the surface everything was fine but underneath she was always waiting for the ice to crack and plunge her into the icy water of disaster.

She rubbed absently at her aching breasts and then realised what she was doing. What on earth was wrong with the stupid things? Maybe it was the weight she was putting on—too many regular meals, too much rich food. It was time she went to a doctor. But look on the bright side, she reflected; at least you weren't pregnant. Not that she had had much literal proof to the contrary, but a few tiny spots of that very light period had released her from her growing anxiety.

As she sprang upright a wave of dizziness left her light-headed. Stress, she decided. Rico was bad for her nerves. Stupid of her to start a row on the phone, though, especially when he wouldn't be coming home until tomorrow. But then she had had every right to be angry. Rico had no right to ride roughshod over her wishes. Maybe he was keen to make her more socially acceptable, she thought bitterly. His live-in partner, the artist... no longer an undiscovered talent.

Face it, she conceded abruptly, you're really hurt that he didn't invite you to Edinburgh. It was so ridiculous too. Couldn't she bear him to be out of her sight for even twenty-four hours? But whereas three and a half weeks ago, feeling as she did now, she would have cheerfully and spontaneously invited herself along the same period had reduced her ability to be that bold. Being careful was inhibiting. She snatched up a piece of charcoal and her sketch-pad and drew a caricature of Rico, complete with grinning bimbo on his arm, festooned in jewellery that resembled chains.

So they had had a fight. Fights were not infrequent, she had to admit. How had she ever thought they had nothing in common? Her mouth twisted. Both of them were stubborn, quick-tempered and bossy. But neither of them was prone to holding spite. They were both crazy about horses and they spent an awful lot of time together without ever getting bored. It had been like a honeymoon—two people wrapped up in each other to the exclusion of the rest of the world. She would keep that thought to herself. She was well aware that he was throwing the party to introduce her to his friends.

Late that afternoon Haversham announced a second visitor. Bella looked up from the magazine she had been somewhat sleepily studying and was astonished to see Griff bearing down on her.

'Getting in here is like getting into Fort Knox,' he complained grimly. 'And as for getting the phone number... forget it. That is highly confidential information!'

Bella stood up with a frown. 'What are you doing here?'

'I'm not here by choice.' He sighed. 'Look, if Hector had had a note of the phone number I wouldn't be here—'

'Hector?'

'My boss is Hector's solicitor.' He reminded her of the connection through which they had met. 'I'm afraid the old boy's had a heart attack.'

Bella stared at him in mute horror and swayed sickly.

'Steady on.' Griff pushed her back down on the seat she had vacated. 'You're really fond of the old buzzard,' he muttered in surprise. 'He's not dead but he's not too good from what I understand.'

Afterwards Bella could never recall that drive to London with Griff. She spent the whole journey spinning between awful guilt and simple prayer. Had it been her decision to live with Rico which had prompted this? She had only seen Hector twice since then and he had still been trying to persuade her to leave Rico.

'He *is* seventy-eight,' the sister in Intensive Care told her quietly. 'If he's still with us in the morning, he has a chance.'

'I thought he was only about seventy,' Bella mumbled thickly through her tears.

'You can sit with him for a while. You're the only person he asked for.'

'I'll wait out here,' Griff said resignedly.

She had forgotten about him. Awkwardly she turned to thank him for driving her to the hospital. 'But don't wait for me. I won't leave until...well, until I see how it goes,' she completed tautly.

Hector looked so frail, so shrunken lying in the railed bed. She covered his hand with hers, willed him to feel her presence, and sat there, gripped by the awareness that she had been far closer to Hector than she had ever been to her grandfather. Hector had understood her in a way her mother's father never had.

In the early evening Hector's solicitor, Mr Harvey, arrived. He gave her the keys to the house and mentioned, with a cloaked look, that if Hector made it out of Intensive Care he would be moved to a private room, and then to a convalescent home. Those were Hector's wishes as laid down by him in the event of serious illness.

'He'll hate that.' Bella sighed, refusing to believe that Hector would not live to see those wishes carried out. 'What about his relatives? Why aren't they here?'

'Hector didn't want them told,' the solicitor admitted. 'But I have informed them. They said that they would keep in touch with the situation by phone.'

It was a very long night. Around dawn Hector opened his eyes on Bella and smiled. Then, after weakly squeezing her hand, he drifted away again. She bought herself breakfast in the cafeteria.

She needed sleep. Accepting that reality, she caught a bus back to Hector's house. She was in the act of wearily climbing the steps when a hand came out of nowhere and snatched the key from her grasp. She spun round.

'Rico!' she gasped in consternation, pressing a hand to her palpitating heart. 'What a fright you gave me!'

He unlocked the door, pushed it back and thrust her inside. Slamming it, he rested back against it and released his breath in a hiss. His eyes were slivers of raw gold condemnation in his dark, set face. 'You little bitch,' he muttered raggedly.

'I beg your pardon?' Reeling with exhaustion and shock at his sudden appearance, Bella slumped down on the stairs and focused on him with dazed eyes.

'*Por qué*...why?' he slammed at her with unhidden savagery.

She could feel the violence in him, coiled up tight like a cobra ready to strike. He was struggling to contain it, on the edge. Her brain was moving in slow motion, could not yet comprehend what on earth was the matter with him. 'Rico...I—'

'Don't try to lie to me!' he grated with vicious bite. 'You've been out all night. You're still wearing the clothes you had on at breakfast yesterday. *Madre de Dios*, I trusted you, I actually trusted you! But I make one wrong move and you react like a whore—'

'A whore?' She framed the words with the greatest of difficulty, scrutinising him with wide, incredulous eyes.

Outraged by her lack of response, Rico reached for her with hard hands and hauled her upright. 'You thought I wouldn't find out, *es verdad*?' he seethed down at her in a blaze of fury, his diction destroyed by the thickness of his accent. 'You would've told me that you came up to see Hector and stayed the night here. If I hadn't seen you coming back this morning I wouldn't have known that you had been with Atherton all night!'

The penny finally dropped with Bella. Her stomach heaved with nausea. 'The butler talked,' she said with heavy irony. 'He told you that I left Winterwood with Griff.'

As Rico released her with a vicious burst of Spanish she slumped back down again, feeling really ill. That Rico could believe for one second that she could be that treacherous, that disloyal and that *cheap* filled her with shrinking distaste.

When she spoke it was more like talking to herself than to Rico. 'I meant to phone last night and leave a message for you but I was so upset that I forgot. It didn't even occur to me that you would distrust me to this extent... that you *could*... Dear God.' Bella groaned, staggering upright on a wave of nausea more powerful than any she had yet managed to ride out and heading blindly for the sanctuary of the downstairs cloakroom, 'I've been sleeping with a stranger...

'"I kiss'd thee ere I kill'd thee,"' she mumbled in a daze as she yanked open the door. '"He was a gentleman on whom I built An absolute trust."'

'*Othello* and *Macbeth*,' Rico growled in incredulous recognition. His bewilderment and frustration unconcealed, he simply stood there glowering at her. The phone started ringing. Neither of them paid it any heed.

To the accompaniment of the phone shrilling, Bella just managed to shut the door before she was horribly sick. As someone who had always rejoiced in an iron digestive system, she was shaken by her own bodily weakness. Afterwards she clung to the sink and rinsed her mouth out. At least the phone had finally stopped.

The door opened. 'Go away,' she said thickly.

'The phone,' Rico breathed tautly. 'It's some cousin of Hector's. He wants to know what hospital Hector's in... He's waiting for an answer.'

Bella swallowed hard and gave the answer, then listened dully to him concluding the call.

'How bad is it?' Rico murmured even more tautly. '*Dios*, you look terrible—'

He was a quick study. Reasoning had returned, suggesting the real explanation for her overnight absence. Bella wished that the call hadn't come. She would have left Rico to stew in his own vile assumptions. He didn't deserve to be let off the hook this quickly and this easily.

This was the male she had sacrificed her dreams for, the male she had burnt her rulebook over... and where had it got her? Maybe exactly where she deserved to be.

'Bella, Hector's *not*...?'

'No, he's still hanging in there.' As she spoke he attempted to curve an arm round her. Jerking dizzily away and grabbing hold of the banister, she gasped, 'Leave me alone!'

Ignoring her demand, Rico closed his arms round her from behind. 'Forgive me,' he said tightly.

She was too physically weak to fight him. 'Why can't you just go? I've been at the hospital all night and I'm not in the mood for you or any of this... It's probably my fault he's in there in the first place!' she completed with a stifled sob, her hand flying up to her wobbling mouth.

'It couldn't possibly be your fault.'

'He was upset when I moved in with you!' she slung at him shakily.

She heard him expel his breath.

'Oh, just go away,' she mumbled, barely able to stand, she felt so faint.

'I'm not leaving you like this. I'll take you back to my apartment—'

'I'm staying here.'

Rico swept her up into his arms. 'You're not well. You can't stay here alone. You should be in bed.'

'Someone should be here to answer the phone—'

'Not you in the condition you're in,' Rico spelt out.

He carried her out to the limo and there was nothing she could do to prevent him. All her concentration was bent on holding back the sick wooziness that was afflicting her. She would be all right once she had a couple of hours' sleep but she could not understand why her body was letting her down so badly. Had she caught some bug? Worse, could she have put Hector at risk by sitting with him? She had never felt so drained in her entire life.

When they reached the spacious apartment Bella crawled straight into bed. She had nothing to wear. Rico produced a silk pyjama jacket which she donned in silence. He said that he had called a doctor—a friend of his in the private sector—who had consulting rooms just down the street. Dully she nodded, relieved to notice that her nausea was beginning to recede.

'Maybe it was something you ate,' Rico suggested stiltedly.

She said nothing.

He sank down on the foot of the bed, searching her pinched profile. 'Bella . . . we'd had a row,' he reminded her in a tense undertone. 'When I heard you'd gone off with Atherton naturally I was disturbed.'

'The senior partner in Griff's firm is Hector's solicitor. He put Griff in charge of informing me about Hector's heart attack. Griff had to drive all the way down to Winterwood because he couldn't find out the phone number.'

'How could I have known of that connection?'

'It doesn't matter. I haven't given you any grounds for thinking that I would behave like a tart,' she muttered tightly. 'I'm not your ex-wife and I won't take the heat for her.'

'I made a mistake,' he acknowledged tautly.

Bella felt horribly confused. Deep down inside she knew that she was going to forgive him but somehow she just couldn't bring herself to tell him that yet.

Loving someone who did not love you was an unrewarding road to humiliation, she reflected miserably. His distrust had bitten deep, hurting her badly at a moment when she was already struggling to cope. With Rico she had no defensive shell, and part of her deeply resented that vulnerability. She wanted to make him suffer and she was ashamed of that fact. How could you try to punish someone for not loving you?

'Two mistakes,' Rico adjusted flatly in the continuing silence. 'I shouldn't have asked Dai to call. But it seemed such a waste—all those fabulous paintings piling up. I'm proud of what you can do with that brush.'

His weight left the mattress. Bella curved her face into the pillow, tears stinging her eyes. What a bitch she was! She was in the act of stretching out a forgiving hand when she heard the door open, the murmur of an unfamiliar voice. The doctor had arrived.

He told her to call him George. He had one of those wonderfully round faces which instilled good cheer. Rico had barely left the room when Bella found herself sitting up and reeling off her symptoms with the subdued irritation of someone who was rarely ill. She submitted to an examination and answered one or two questions which struck her as highly irrelevant when she was suffering from a stomach disorder. But no doubt George knew his business better than she did.

'You're pregnant,' he finally delivered very quietly.

Bella changed her mind about him knowing his business. 'No way,' she told him, with a forced laugh at such an insane diagnosis.

'Bella, I'm a consultant gynaecologist,' he returned gently. 'And if I'm wrong I ought to be back in medical school. First pregnancies in particular carry unmistakable signs. You are at least two months pregnant.'

'But I had a—' she began jerkily.

He explained that sometimes what he described as a partially suppressed period could occur. Bella went into cold shock while he talked to her about not pushing herself too hard and taking proper rest.

'Don't tell him!' she begged abruptly.

He reminded her of patient confidentiality and she apologised, so shattered by what he had told her that she could hardly think straight. He paused at the door, clearly troubled by her reaction.

'Bella, Rico's very fond of children. You should see him with mine,' he said ruefully.

So Rico liked other people's children. What did that mean? Feeling weak, she lay down again. Her hand slid down unsteadily to her still flat stomach. She struggled to accept that there was a baby growing inside her—a baby conceived weeks ago while she had been convincing herself that no such conception *could* take place.

She had been as foolishly naïve as an uninformed teenager, she realised. There was no such thing as a failsafe time to make love. There was always a risk. And Rico had ironically been far more concerned by the possibility than she had been . . . probably because it was the very last thing he wanted to happen.

The door opened.

'George was very cagey,' Rico said impatiently.

'It's just a stupid stomach upset—probably that breakfast I ate at the hospital,' Bella volunteered, and forced herself to turn over and meet his enquiring gaze. 'I'm glad it wasn't anything that could have put Hector at risk of infection. Now all I want to do is sleep.'

Just looking at Rico suddenly tore her heart in two. She searched his strong, dark face, read the relief there, and knew she deserved an Oscar for her performance— but then it was wonderful what fear could do. It sharpened the wits and in the short term chose deception over honesty. She wasn't ready yet to share such devastating news, was already wondering how she would ever bring herself to share it.

'I'll go back to the hospital in the afternoon,' she added, dropping her head back down on the pillow as if she were too exhausted to stay awake.

She closed her eyes, knowing that it would take a miracle for sleep to overcome her now. For it was over— she and Rico—over, finished, *destroyed*. Fate had had

the last laugh of all. Secure in the belief that there was
no question of her being pregnant, Rico had been
brutally frank. A baby was a complication he did not
want. She told herself that she was lucky to know his
true feelings on the subject. Who could tell how he might
have felt forced to react if she had discovered that she
was pregnant a month ago?

Certainly he wouldn't have felt disposed to offer marriage, but he might well have felt that sensitivity demanded that he conceal just how appalled he was by the
news. She didn't want pretences like that between them.
Honesty was always the best policy, but oh, God, how
it could hurt sometimes . . .

She drove back the pain consuming her, calling herself
a coward. Their affair would have burnt out on his side
anyway sooner or later. Now it would just happen sooner
and she would be the one to make the break. She had
no choice.

Just as Cleo had once made Bella welcome—a child
unplanned and unsupported by any man—Bella would
do the same for *her* child. It was that simple. But she
felt horribly guilty. How could she have been so reckless?
Whenever she had thought of becoming a mother she
had always believed that the event would take place
within a stable, loving relationship.

By three in the afternoon Bella was up again under
her own steam. Incredibly she had dozed off. She
showered and changed into the fresh clothes which she
had flung into an overnight bag the previous day at
Winterwood. Physically she felt much better but inside
herself she felt dead.

She had woken up with the knowledge of what she
had to do. Break it off, finish it . . . get it over with!
Hector's illness and her argument with Rico, which now
seemed so pitifully unimportant, had supplied a natural
break. When she came back from the hospital this
evening she would tell him.

Since she had assumed that he was back at the bank, it was a shock when Rico strode out of the drawing room as she was heading for the hall. She froze, shielding her startled eyes with her lashes.

'You were in the shower when I came to wake you up. How do you feel?'

'Fine now,' she said stiffly.

'I've ordered a light meal for you.'

'Thanks, but I'm—'

'Bella, be sensible.' He pressed her into the dining room where a place for one was already laid at the gleaming table. 'You have to try to eat something. Hector's fine, by the way. You don't need to rush.'

His manservant appeared out of nowhere and a beautifully cooked omelette was slid in front of her. Her hands trembled as she reached out for the knife and fork. 'I thought you'd be at the bank,' she said once the man had gone.

'I took the afternoon off.'

She couldn't eat; she just couldn't eat. She replaced the cutlery again, studied the table with anguished eyes and then cleared her throat. 'You remember we decided on seeing how it went for a month?' she whispered in a rush. 'Well, it's not working for me any more and I think you must feel—'

'Eat before I force-feed you,' Rico broke in, as if he were talking to a difficult child.

Bella stood up and backed away from the table. 'Rico, listen to me,' she muttered tightly, crossing her arms and turning away from him, unable to stay still. 'This is nothing to do with those stupid arguments we had . . . please believe that. But sometimes a crisis makes you see more clearly—'

'You're so blind right now, *gatita*,' Rico interposed in the same indulgent tone, 'that you'd fall over your own feet. Our relationship has nothing to do with Hector's heart attack.'

'That isn't what I was going to say!' she protested, in so much turmoil that she couldn't even keep her voice steady. Involuntarily her look clashed with steady dark eyes and she hurriedly averted her gaze again. 'The point is... The point is,' she repeated doggedly, 'that two months ago we were kidnapped, and in the grip of that trauma sex got involved and—'

'Sex got involved the first time I laid eyes on you,' he proffered without shame. 'The trauma of being kidnapped had nothing to do with it.'

Bella ignored that. She didn't trust herself to look at him, couldn't afford to be tempted. 'What I realise now is that we sort of became dependent on each other in that container, and I don't want to be dependent any more. I want my freedom back.'

'I might be more impressed if you looked me in the face and told me that,' he drawled with derision.

Bella looked up, blocked him out, a terrible pain scything through her. 'It's over. I'm sorry but that's the way it is.'

'You are one lousy liar,' Rico said grimly, crossing the room in one long, menacing stride. 'What the hell is going on here?'

Before he could reach her Bella dived for the door. In seconds she was out of the apartment and into the mercifully waiting lift. She made it out onto the busy street at speed. Sobs were tearing at her convulsing throat. She dashed her hand across her streaming eyes, devastated by the force of her emotions. Then she drew in a deep, slow breath and walked on down the street.

CHAPTER TEN

AN HOUR later Bella was sitting by Hector's bedside with the fixed expression of someone in shock and striving to hide it. He had already been moved out of Intensive Care and into a private room. But while she had been asleep at the apartment Rico had visited him.

'Absolute nonsense for you to think my dicky heart had anything to do with your love life,' Hector was telling her in reproof. 'I had an attack three years ago, as you very well know. As for you and Rico... well, times have changed and he seems very fond of you—'

'Fond of me?'

'Why else would he invite me to Winterwood to convalesce?'

'He's done what?' she squeaked, shattered by the news.

'I must say I'm really looking forward to seeing the house again.' He sighed fondly. 'When it belonged to the Cliffords in the fifties I was a regular visitor there—'

'But I thought you were planning on a convalescent home?'

'Rico told me what that would cost.' Weak as he was, Hector all but shuddered in recollection.

'How clever... I mean, how *conscientious* of him to have found out for you,' she managed with the greatest difficulty. 'But I could look after you at home if you like.'

'Not with that showing at the Matheison Gallery coming up. I wouldn't dream of it.'

Bella's nails dug into her palms like talons. Ten minutes with Hector had sent her from utter despondency to sheer rage. Rico had trussed her up like a goose ready for the oven! Perfectly well aware that their relationship was in deep water, he had ensured that it would be virtually impossible for her to move out. Hector was positively looking forward to a break in the country which would cost him not a penny and where he would be waited on hand and foot.

How could she now announce that she had broken up with Rico? That was no longer the news which she had innocently imagined would cheer Hector up. Indeed, she had the hideous suspicion that Hector, who liked very few people, had decided to make an exception of Rico.

As he drifted off to sleep he was mumbling about what ingenious ideas Rico had on the enthralling subject of reducing expenditure and making the most of a small income. Fit to be tied, Bella stalked out of the room.

She found Rico standing in the small waiting area at the end of the corridor. He watched her striding towards him with supreme cool.

'You devious toe-rag!' she launched at him from ten feet away.

'"A slippery and subtle knave,"' Rico murmured smoothly.

'Don't you dare quote Shakespeare at me!' she hissed in fury. 'How could you use an old man like that...how *could* you?'

'If you don't lower your voice, I shall treat you exactly as if you were the child you are choosing to emulate,' he drawled in a whiplash tone. 'Now take a deep breath and calm down...*right now.*'

Her outraged eyes shimmered. She buttoned her mouth shut, not trusting herself to speak. She wanted to slap him and he knew it and he wasn't impressed. Flinging her a grim glance, he stood back for her to enter the waiting lift.

'We'll talk in the car,' he told her.

Bella shot into the back seat of the limousine like a spitting cat, temper still blazing through her. 'How dare—?'

'Be silent,' Rico said sharply. 'You cannot make accusations of that variety and expect to get away with it. Hector Barsay may not be a blood relative but you are very attached to him. Since he was also a friend of my late father's for many years, I naturally felt that I should visit him.'

Gritting her teeth, she studied her tightly clenched hands. So far, so good, but there was no way he could explain himself out of what he had done during that visit.

'When I saw him earlier you were sulking—'

'I do not sulk—'

'You sulk,' Rico assured her. 'We had had an argument, but when I went to that hospital I had no idea that when I returned to the apartment you would announce that our relationship was at an end.'

Bella swallowed hard. It was a point she had to concede.

'Hector doesn't want to go to a home where he will be surrounded by strangers. He also misses you a great deal. That I should offer him hospitality was a natural progression from those facts. At Winterwood he will have every comfort but he will also have the privacy which is so important to him.'

'All right, I'm sorry,' Bella muttered from between clenched teeth. 'But where does that leave us now?'

'You appear to have already made that decision,' Rico retorted drily. 'I gather you didn't tell him the truth?'

'How could I?' she demanded fiercely.

'Especially when you would have looked a little stupid when I'd told him that you were staying put.'

She looked at him for the first time. 'I beg your pardon?'

Hooded dark eyes rested intently on her. 'You've been crying. Your nose is still pink.'

'Thank you so much for telling me,' she mumbled in a wobbly voice, suddenly feeling tearful again and ready to scream at the hormonal upheaval of pregnancy. Of course, that was what was the matter with her.

'We're going back to Winterwood,' he informed her.

'I'm going back to Hector's house.'

'I have the keys. I'm not giving them to you until you calm down.'

'I am perfectly calm,' Bella bit out furiously. 'Give me those keys! I don't know what I'm going to do when Hector comes out of hospital but that has to be a few weeks away and I'll deal with it then!'

'You're not getting those keys.'

'And you call *me* childish?'

But he didn't answer her. Her throat was thick with clogged tears. Defensively she turned her head away again. In a sense this was all her own fault. Back at the apartment she had not been prepared to face Rico. She had not had time to work out what she needed to say to sound convincing.

In short, she had made a mess of telling him that their relationship was over—so great a mess that he thought that she was simply being pathetically immature and vindictive over that argument in spite of his apologies. He did not believe that she really wanted to break off their affair.

And, since the truth was that she *didn't*, it really wasn't that surprising that Rico should think that way. Walking away from the man she loved demanded a degree of detachment and acting ability which Bella now acknowledged she did not possess. It was going to take lies to convince Rico that she had meant what she said. Maybe she ought to tell him that she had realised yesterday that she still had feelings for Griff... or maybe she should just tell him the truth.

No, not yet, she decided tautly. That would be a truth more easily dealt with when they were no longer together.

As she headed for the stairs in the echoing hall at Winterwood Rico murmured, 'I expect you to come down to dinner.'

Bella almost exploded. He had tied her up in knots with Hector, forced her to return to Winterwood and he was withholding the keys to Hector's house. He had been treating her like a fractious toddler on the brink of a temper tantrum from the minute she'd walked out of Hector's room!

She spun round. 'Tough!'

'It'll be Haversham's turn to laugh if I have to carry you downstairs,' Rico warned her.

'You wouldn't dare.' But she knew he would, knew she could push him so far and no further. Biting her tongue, green eyes blazing, Bella looked back at him, thwarted.

'Don't wear that figure-hugging black velvet dress,' he murmured softly. 'I don't like it.'

'I'll wear whatever the hell I want!'

And from the minute Bella got out of the shower she knew it would be that dress which she put on. Only, the zip proved oddly reluctant to go up. When she finally got it up and turned to look in the mirror she realised why. Her breasts now foamed over the straining neckline like overripe fruits. She looked down at them in horror and attempted to squash them down again. It was a pointless exercise. Until that moment she really hadn't appreciated just how much her shape had already changed.

Coming down the staircase in a relentlessly shapeless floral dress which had been a fashion accident, Bella found herself wondering why Rico had told her *not* to wear that black dress. He had only ever seen her in it twice and the second time, weeks ago, he had told her she looked stunning in it.

He was waiting for her in the drawing room. Tall, dark and spectacularly handsome, he surveyed her entrance. Her heart skipped a beat; her mouth went dry. In mute misery she swerved her attention off him again.

'That dress looks like a maternity outfit,' he drawled.

Bella flinched and spilt some of the sherry which Haversham always served her before dinner and which she had yet to drink. But, since the same thought about the dress had occurred to her, she thought nothing of the remark. She contrived a shrug and said, 'It's comfortable.'

'Allow me to get you another drink,' Rico said.

'No, I'm not really— Oh, dinner!' she exclaimed with relief, rising to her feet as Haversham appeared.

Since she was really hungry, she was on the second course before it crossed her mind that it was time to bite the bullet and convince Rico that their affair was over. So far the meal had been unusually silent. And that, now that she actually thought about it, was strange. Rico was not, as a rule, someone who quietly smouldered. Rico did not suffer in silence. Yet, in spite of emitting hostile vibrations into the steadily thickening atmosphere between them, he had barely opened his mouth.

'Why are you so quiet?'

He sent her a glimmering smile which made her feel uncomfortable. 'I wanted to see you eat a decent meal.'

'Like the condemned man?' Bella looked across the table at him and steeled herself. 'I'm afraid I wasn't very honest with you this afternoon...'

He tautened perceptibly. His narrowed dark eyes rested on her with grim intensity. He drained his glass of wine and set it down without taking his attention from her once. 'I am aware of that fact.'

For some peculiar reason Bella felt as though the dining-table between them had just become a bank manager's desk, with her playing the role of debtor asking for a loan that was about to be refused. There was just something so cold and businesslike about Rico's attitude.

'Well, I owe you the truth,' she told him.

'You do,' he agreed.

'I've realised that I still have feelings for Griff,' she muttered, and she didn't need to pretend to feel guilty saying that; she *did* feel guilty.

The silence stretched like a rubber band pulled to breaking-point. Then Rico's strong face clenched, his sensual mouth flattening into a bloodless line. 'To employ your jargon...tough!'

Bella gave him a dazed look, wildly disconcerted by such a response.

'Why don't you tell me the *rest* of the truth?' he invited softly, only there was something innately menacing about that tone.

'I don't know what you're talking about.'

'Maybe you could tell me why you're not wearing your black dress...or why you've sworn off alcohol again?' Rico invited. 'Or why one of my closest friends can't meet my eyes when I ask him a perfectly reasonable question?'

Bella had turned pale.

'Or how about why you're developing a bosom worthy of a *Playboy* centrefold?'

'How dare you?' she gasped, unable to dredge anything more riveting from a brain in the deep freeze of turmoil. He couldn't possibly have guessed, she told herself frantically; he couldn't possibly have!

Rico vented a harsh laugh and thrust his plate away. 'You're pregnant...and all I want to know now is *how* pregnant?'

In a wave of pain Bella bowed her head.

'George didn't tell me but when you got up out of that bed and told me we were finished *you* told me,' Rico spelt out. 'I can add two and two. So tell me, when did this happy event take place?'

'When we were kidnapped—'

'So now I discover *why* you suddenly agreed to move in with me!' he shot at her.

'I didn't know until today!' she protested, shocked that he could think that.

'And with the best will in the world how am I supposed to believe that?' he breathed, sounding almost weary.

'Because it's the truth.'

'For someone who prides herself on telling the truth, and who gives an outstanding impression of always delivering it, you tell a lot of lies!'

A sob was trapped in her throat. Why, oh, why hadn't she had the wit to tell him this afternoon as soon as she'd found out? But she knew why. This was the very scene she had sought to avoid and it was tearing her apart. She had believed that a few weeks or months down the line, when they had already split up, she would have been able to handle his bitter reaction a lot more easily. But in avoiding the issue she had only made Rico more suspicious.

The tip of her tongue stole out to moisten her dry lips. She lifted her vibrant head. 'I can't blame you 'for thinking that, but I just wasn't ready to face this yet. I was as shocked as you are and I knew how you would feel—'

'*Por Dios*, you have not a clue how I feel!' he raked back at her.

Bella forced herself to explain why she had assumed that she was not pregnant, and at that moment did not much care whether Rico believed her or not. They had both taken that risk two months earlier, and if the first time their lovemaking had been prompted by her, the second time Rico had been the guilty party. The responsibility cut both ways.

'And what are your plans now—a termination?' he demanded abruptly.

She looked back at him in horror.

'I had to ask,' he murmured tautly, and oddly enough her unspoken rejection of such an option seemed to remove much of the strain stamped into his bronzed features. 'I was afraid that that was your intention.'

'No,' she confirmed, decidedly knocked off balance by his reaction because deep down inside she had been equally afraid that that might have been *his* intention.

'I would not have allowed that,' Rico added, just in case she hadn't got the message.

'And I wouldn't have considered it,' she asserted tightly.

'We will get married as soon as possible.'

Bella very nearly fell off her chair. Wide-eyed, she stared back at him, refusing to believe that he had simply murmured that statement as if it almost went without saying that they should now get married, as if any other response to their predicament was not even to be considered.

Rico dealt her shocked face a look of granite-hard determination untinged by any amusement. 'I intend to have full legal rights over this child.'

Bella unglued her tongue from the roof of her mouth. Just minutes ago he had told her that she didn't have a clue how he felt about her being pregnant. Now she was tasting the literal truth of that assurance. 'But—'

'Let's go into the drawing room,' he suggested drily, rising fluidly from his seat. 'I doubt that either of us is likely to eat any more tonight.'

Once there, Bella sank down into an armchair. 'How can you talk about marriage?' she whispered helplessly. 'I thought you didn't even like children—'

'When did I ever say that?'

'You said you had no desire to become a father.'

'Naturally not . . . outside marriage,' he stressed.

She was shaken by the simplicity of that clarification.

'As it happens, I am very fond of children,' he breathed tautly as he poured himself a brandy. 'But children make you vulnerable. I had a son once and I lost him again. It was an experience I did not wish to repeat.'

'I'm not sure I understand.' He was talking about the child he had had with his ex-wife.

'His name was Carlos.' Rico sent her a brooding look, his tension palpable. 'And to this day I do not know whether or not he was my child. But it really didn't matter because when he was born I believed he was and I loved him,' he proffered tightly. 'He was the only good thing to come out of a rotten marriage, the only reason I tried so hard to make the marriage work.

'Margarita didn't give a damn about him. He was simply the means by which she married money. But when it came to the divorce he was also the means by which she hoped to achieve a very large settlement.'

All at once Bella was seeing how wildly off-centre her own assumptions had been. 'I wish you had told me this sooner.'

'When Margarita moved out she took Carlos with her. She expected me to buy him back,' he muttered harshly, his jaw clenching. 'But she wanted more than I could afford to pay *then*. When I didn't pay up she lost her head and told everyone that he wasn't mine anyway—'

'How could she do that to you?' Bella whispered.

'The reality was that she didn't know whether he was or not. I had not been her only lover at the time of his conception. Her claim threw the custody battle into chaos, causing a delay in the giving of the judge's decision. Tests had to be carried out. Carlos remained with Margarita and...' he hesitated and gave an almost clumsy shrug '... one day when she was partying he fell into a swimming pool and drowned.'

'Oh, God,' Bella mumbled in shock.

'He was eighteen months old,' Rico revealed curtly. 'And she wasn't fit to have the charge of him. She had had a row with his nanny and sacked her the day before. He didn't have a hope in hell.'

'I'm so sorry.' She swallowed back the tears that were threatening and watched the carpet swim instead. She was appalled by what he had told her.

'And I swore I would never have another child because losing Carlos was the toughest challenge I have ever had to face.' His facial muscles locked, he downed his brandy in one. 'But be assured that now you carry my baby inside you *everything* changes...'

'Yes.' Her head was aching from the tension he had induced.

'We do the very best we can for that baby,' he informed her with sudden savage ferocity. 'And I will not allow you to walk away as Margarita did and take that child from me! He or she is as much mine as yours...and the sooner you accept that reality the better!'

'I don't want to walk away,' Bella said thickly just as the door closed. She looked up. Rico had gone. She flew to her feet and went after him, but by the time she realised that he had left the house and not just gone into another room he had already driven off.

She was distraught and yet part of her wanted to kick him for not telling her about Carlos sooner. It wasn't her fault that she had made a series of false suppositions on the subject of how he felt about children, it was *his*. Yet she understood why he hadn't told her as well. Understandably, talking about that tragedy really upset him. Dear God, what an evil bitch he had married, she thought helplessly.

At first she planned to sit up and wait for him and explain how she had misunderstood. But then she began to go back over all that Rico had said. Marriage hadn't been on his agenda because he hadn't wanted to risk having another child with any woman. Once bitten, twice

shy. But the fact that a baby was actually on the way
had completely altered his attitude.

And he wasn't worried about losing *her*, was he? It
was a bitter irony. Rico was more worried about losing
control of the new life in her womb! No wonder he had
relaxed when he'd realised there was to be no threat of
a termination. Rico, whether he realised it or not, could
not *wait* to get his paws on her baby! He was even prepared to marry her to ensure that he had greater legal
rights!

She went up to bed, deeply shaken and deeply hurt.
She was distressed by what he had told her about Carlos
but never in her entire life had she felt more rejected.
Regardless of the fact that Rico really seemed to want
their child, he seemed to have pitched their relationship
right out the window. And she just couldn't comprehend why it was happening that way.

He woke her up coming to bed. It was some unholy
hour of the morning and he was humming under his
breath. She couldn't believe it. Her teeth clenched. And
when, ten seconds after he got into bed, a pair of arms
reached for her she presented him with a back as welcoming as Everest in a blizzard.

'I asked you to marry me. I thought you'd be pleased,'
he murmured without any expression at all.

Bella shot upright as if he had stabbed her with a knife.
'Why the hell would I be pleased?'

'It *is* what you wanted at the beginning.'

'I wised up!' she screeched.

A lamp was switched on. 'Calm down,' he instructed.
'How do you think that baby feels listening to you
scream?'

'It's listening to you too... being totally, hatefully ob-
jectionable!' she sobbed, her every worst fear about the
exact nature of her value to him now confirmed.

He enclosed her in his arms. She did her stick of
rock impression.

'Bella...' he said tautly. 'I was under a lot of strain earlier. I felt incredibly confused. I was scared that you *were* pregnant... and then scared that you might *not* be! But by the time I was cracking open the champagne with George...' Bella froze in absolute disbelief at this revelation of how he had passed his time away from her '...I realised how extraordinarily happy I feel about this baby,' he delivered with positive fervour, in the tone of someone who believed that he was telling her exactly what she wanted to hear.

'You've been *celebrating* with my doctor?' Bella enunciated in a voice which shook.

'Naturally we did not discuss you either medically or personally,' Rico assured her.

'You *toad*!' she spat.

Rico dropped his air of insouciance and compressed his lips, his glittering golden eyes splintering into hers. 'Do you really think he'll still want you when you tell him you're pregnant?'

'Who?' Bella looked blank.

'*Who?*' Rico echoed, cuttingly incredulous.

Comprehension assailed her. A heady tide of pink washed over her complexion. Somehow, in all the turmoil of the evening, she had forgotten telling him that lie about Griff. Since it now seemed pointless to continue it, she muttered, 'I made that up—'

'*Qué dices?*'

'About Griff... that was a little white lie—'

'"A *little* white lie"?' Rico thundered, springing out of bed. '*Madre de Dios*... you tell me you're in love with another man and you call that "a little white lie"?'

'I had to give you a reason for leaving!' Bella protested.

'So if you are not pining for Biff why *were* you leaving?' he slung at her with a positively feral snarl as he began to get dressed.

'Because of the baby.' Bella gave him an 'are you stupid?' look of angry reproof. 'I thought you wouldn't want it ... I thought it would be the worst news you had ever heard—'

'And when was I going to hear this news?' he roared at her.

'Some time after we'd split up... when the subject wasn't so emotive.'

Rico sent her a glimmering glance of disbelief.

'When it felt less ... personal,' she floundered in desperation.

His disbelief was magnified.

'Does that really make sense to you, *gatita*?' he enquired gently.

Reluctantly she shook her head. In retrospect it didn't make sense. Finding out that she was pregnant had made her panic. She had not been thinking clearly about what she was doing. 'I guess I was running away. I couldn't work up the courage to tell you something I thought you didn't want to hear.'

'And that was my fault?'

Bella shrugged. 'You didn't want to be trapped into marriage again. That's fine.' She took a deep breath. 'But I don't want to marry you on that same basis, Rico. Even though both of us were reckless—'

'I'm never reckless, *gatita*. I knew the risk and I accepted it. I should have known then that there was something special between us...'

Bella winced. 'Rico, you would tell me just about anything to persuade me to marry you. I can understand that but—' A hand had closed round her arm. Rico was pulling her out of bed. 'What are you doing?'

'I want to show you something.'

'It's four o'clock in the morning!'

But he wasn't listening to her. He thrust her robe at her and tossed her mules across to her. 'Come on.'

'Where?'

'You'll see.' Impatiently he propelled her out of the bedroom and downstairs.

When he climbed into the Bugatti outside she hissed, 'I'm not dressed!'

'We're not leaving the estate.'

He drove down the lane that ran from the stable block out to the fields. At the end of it he parked, leaving the headlights on, and walked over to the fence. Thoroughly exasperated by now, Bella leapt out and followed.

'Keep your eyes peeled for something vaguely animate that reminds you of a very tatty, small, moving hearth rug.'

A shape ambled out of the darkness, attracted by the light.

'I located him five days ago,' Rico murmured. 'He hasn't been very well looked after but the vet says he'll be fine once he's groomed and fattened up.'

Bella was already striving to climb the fence, somewhat hampered by her flowing nightwear. Rico lifted her over. 'Fiddlesticks,' she whispered shakily, and then surged over the grass to the Shetland pony.

Ten minutes later she was wiping at her eyes, genuinely overcome not just by the reunion with the little pony she had never thought to see again but by the fact that Rico had gone to so much trouble to trace him and give him back to her.

Rico swung her back over the fence. She slid back into the car, still in a happy daze.

'I planned to get a dog and a cat to go with him,' he murmured very tautly. 'And I was also planning to present the three of them to you before the party.'

'Dog...cat...party?' Bella mumbled in helpless repetition.

'You told me that you loved children and wanted a large fluffy dog, a cat and a pony for them,' Rico reminded her stiffly. 'Well, I was ready to supply them.'

She went rigid, understanding finally sinking in. Rico was telling her that at least a week ago he had been ready to give her what he believed she wanted. And all of a sudden, instead of being touched and pleased by the gesture, she felt like screaming. She wanted him to *love* her, not drag her out to a field in the middle of the night and offer her a menagerie!

He dug something from his pocket and handed it to her. 'This is a sample of the invitations I was having printed. It was going to be an engagement party...a surprise,' he breathed in a harsh undertone. 'I took a lot for granted, *es verdad*?'

Bella was reading the invitation, her heartbeat accelerating. Long before he'd known about the baby Rico had intended to ask her to marry him. She sniffed, her eyes stinging. The fear that he only wanted to marry her because of their child was for ever vanquished.

Rico released his breath in a hiss in the continuing silence, seeming not to appreciate that she was stunned by sheer shock. He drove back to the house and switched off the engine. 'Until you told me you wanted to leave me I thought you loved me...'

'I do,' Bella said distractedly.

'Then why the blazes are you sitting there in silence?' he roared at her without warning.

'Sh-shock,' she proffered shakily.

He groaned something in Spanish and brushed her hair back from her cheekbone with a not quite steady hand. 'I was terrified of losing you. When you said you wanted out I saw my whole world falling apart. There was nothing I would not have done to keep you. And I seemed to have no hold on you but the baby.'

'And you were prepared to use that—'

'*Sí*... I never thought that I could love anyone the way I love you.'

Bella threw her head back, her green eyes clinging to the blaze of his possessive golden gaze. 'I fell in love with you in the container.'

Rico cursed as he collided with the gearstick in his attempt to drag her into his arms. Bella giggled and climbed out of the car, watching him make it round the bonnet to her in record time. He swept her up into his arms and kissed her passionately as he carried her back into the house.

Between kisses he talked all the way up the stairs. 'When you collapsed outside the farmhouse I was like a man possessed. I knew I was in love...or that I thought I was in love. But I had no idea that you felt the same way. You are so different from every other woman I know. I was afraid to tell you how I felt in case you laughed...'

'I wouldn't have laughed,' Bella whispered, all choked up from realising that he was vulnerable too.

'I am eleven years older. I feared that you might become bored with me.'

'No chance.'

'I couldn't take my eyes off you the first time I saw you. You didn't even *notice*,' he complained.

'Rico, try being poor and smashing up a Bugatti. I was in shock, and then you started calling the police—'

'And you fell asleep in the limo...as if I wasn't there!'

'Strikes me your ego needed a little challenge.' She dropped her voice an octave and boomed in mocking mimicry, '"I have known women to take tremendous risks to make my acquaintance." What do they do—abseil down the walls of the bank and kick their way in through the windows?' She giggled.

Rico lowered her onto the bed. 'You might as well have done. You came into my life and turned it upside-down. You fascinate me.'

'You fascinate me too.' She reached up to him, found his mouth again and yanked him down to her.

They made love slowly, luxuriating in every sweet sensation.

'Am I allowed to buy you things now?' he asked afterwards. 'Festoon you with jewellery?'

'I want a Porsche,' Bella said out of sheer badness.

His black lashes dropped over his too expressive eyes, but his sudden tension said it all for him. 'No problem. You pass an advanced driving test and I'll buy you one.'

'Just you wait,' Bella told him.

Bella watched Rico swing their daughter up in his arms as he came through the hall. Jenny wrapped her little arms round his throat in a death grip and hugged him, making excitable 'da-da' sounds. He had clearly been affectionately attacked by their wolfhound before he'd even got in the door: there was a large, muddy paw-print on his jacket. Bella grinned as he looked up and their eyes connected over Jenny's dark, curly head—smug green into slightly tense gold.

'You passed...?'

'I passed.'

'Congratulations,' It sounded rather forced. He couldn't help it. The thought of her in a Porsche, empowered by an advanced driving test or otherwise, still brought him out in a cold sweat, she assumed.

Having put Jenny down for a nap, she suggested, 'I'll take you for a spin, shall I?'

'You've already bought it?' Rico breathed, looking shattered.

'It's in the garage.'

Hector was out for his evening stroll down the drive. He waved. Rico had bought his London house for their use and renovated it. The court case which had put their kidnappers into prison was thankfully long behind them now and Hector had decided to rent a cottage on the estate.

When he wasn't playing honorary grandpa for Jenny's benefit, he was fully occupied with thinking up economies for Rico to make at Winterwood. And Rico would listen with that little smile of his and marvel that he had never had such ideas himself. It was just one of the reasons why Bella loved him so much.

Rico peered into the garage with a fixed smile which quickly fell away. 'That's a Volvo estate!'

'I never wanted a Porsche. I'm not that fond of speed,' Bella said gently. 'And this is much more practical for a working artist with a child.'

'You never wanted a Porsche...but you made me jump through all the hoops pretending you did!' Rico was now struggling to look angry, she gathered, instead of painfully relieved.

She reached for his silk tie and tugged him towards her with all the provocativeness of a very confident woman. 'I like to keep you on your toes, Mr da Silva.'

'*Dios mío*, you are not joking,' he growled thickly, crushing her into his arms and kissing her breathless, passion blazing up between them just as it always did. 'And fortunately for you I find it irresistible, because, having phoned Haversham to ascertain your success, at lunchtime I went out and bought you a Porsche.'

Bella's jaw dropped.

'Just think of the mileage Hector is going to get out of conspicuous consumerism like this!' Rico suddenly said, laughing.

HARLEQUIN  PRESENTS®

Watch for the latest story
in our exciting series:

when men find their way to fatherhood by fair means,
by foul or even by default!

Dominic had made it clear that he held Sophie
and baby Ryan responsible for ruining his life!

So why was he asking her to marry him?

#1873 **DOMINIC'S CHILD**
by
Catherine Spencer

Available in March wherever
Harlequin books are sold.

Look us up on-line at: http://www.romance.net

FHTP-3

Take 4 bestselling love stories FREE

Plus get a FREE surprise gift!

Special Limited-time Offer

Mail to Harlequin Reader Service®

3010 Walden Avenue
P.O. Box 1867
Buffalo, N.Y. 14240-1867

YES! Please send me 4 free Harlequin Presents® novels and my free surprise gift. Then send me 6 brand-new novels every month, which I will receive months before they appear in bookstores. Bill me at the low price of $2.90 each plus 25¢ delivery and applicable sales tax, if any*. That's the complete price and a savings of over 10% off the cover prices—quite a bargain! I understand that accepting the books and gift places me under no obligation ever to buy any books. I can always return a shipment and cancel at any time. Even if I never buy another book from Harlequin, the 4 free books and the surprise gift are mine to keep forever.

106 BPA A3UL

Name	(PLEASE PRINT)	
Address	Apt. No.	
City	State	Zip

This offer is limited to one order per household and not valid to present Harlequin Presents® subscribers. *Terms and prices are subject to change without notice. Sales tax applicable in N.Y.

UPRES-696   ©1990 Harlequin Enterprises Limited

HARLEQUIN  PRESENTS®

It shouldn't have been allowed to happen—but it did!

#1872 DESERT MISTRESS
by Helen Bianchin

Kristi's brother was a hostage and only one man could
help: Sheikh Shalef bin Youssef Al-Sayed. He had power
and influence at his fingertips—how could Kristi win his
support? He was way out of her league....

**Available in March wherever
Harlequin books are sold.**

Look us up on-line at: http://www.romance.net   FORB3

Jake wasn't sure why he'd agreed to take the place
of his twin brother, nor why he'd agreed to commit
Nathan's crime. Maybe it was misplaced loyalty.

DANGEROUS
Temptation

by *New York Times* bestselling author

**Anne
MATHER**

After surviving a plane crash, Jake wakes up in a hospital
room and can't remember anything—or anyone...
including one very beautiful woman who comes to see
him. His wife. Caitlin. Who watches him so guardedly.

Her husband seems like a stranger to Caitlin—he's full of
warmth and passion. Just like the man she thought she'd
married. Until his memory returns. And with it, a danger
that threatens them all.

Available in February 1997 at your favorite retail outlet.

MIRA The brightest star in women's fiction   MAMDT

Look us up on-line at: http://www.romance.net

You're About to Become a

Become a

Privileged
Woman

Reap the rewards of fabulous free gifts and
benefits with proofs-of-purchase from
Harlequin and Silhouette books

Pages & Privileges™

It's our way of thanking you for
buying our books at your
favorite retail stores.

**PROOF OF
PURCHASE**

Offer expires March 31, 1997

HP-PP22

Harlequin and Silhouette—
the most privileged readers in the world!

For more information about Harlequin and
Silhouette's PAGES & PRIVILEGES program call the
Pages & Privileges Benefits Desk: 1-503-794-2499

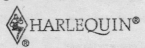

HARLEQUIN®

HP-PP22